SNOWBIRDS

A RECLAIMED HEARTS NOVELLA

ELLE KEATON

ONE

Hatch

"Two hundred and forty damned hours of vacation time. You are officially off the clock as of five minutes ago. This isn't a suggestion, Chris, this is a direct order."

Crap.

Chris Hatch quietly released a breath of air and pinched the bridge of his nose. His boss never called him by his first name unless he was really worried about him. Normally it was Hatch this, Hatch that, Hatch, pull a damn miracle out of your ass. Hatch, save the world. Hatch, rescue the girl tied up on the train tracks before the sun sets.

Chris sniggered and nearly dropped the handset. The conversation wasn't remotely funny, so he must have been more tired than he'd realized.

He'd been with the DEA for almost twenty years, climbing up through the ranks until he'd reached his current position. He had direct authority over a large team of agents—with one recent opening, left by Dante Castone and yet to be filled—as well as responsibilities involving a variety of investigations and agency overlap.

The job was exhausting and a lot like a jigsaw puzzle, except the human pieces didn't stay in place. They moved all over and had to be watched constantly; the face of one specific human came to mind.

"You're flirting with a bad case of burnout."

Fuck. Chris blinked—McBride was *still* talking.

"It's past time for you to take a vacation. If I see—or hear—even a muted whisper about you back at work before those excess hours are used up, we'll be having another discussion."

Chris wanted to point out that they were, in fact, *not* having a discussion. A discussion was the back-and-forth exchange of ideas, not a litany of tyrannical orders from on high. But he kept his mouth shut and instead stared around at the walls of his office while McBride droned on about HR and mental health.

Fucking mental health. His job *was* his mental health.

He *liked* his office. It was comfortable. And, because of its location outside North Portland, he had a partial view of the Mighty Columbia along with the most southern edge of Washington State. He'd often joked that if the uppers knew the strip mall, and thus his office, had a view, they wouldn't have let him keep it. Heaven forbid middle management types like him enjoyed being in their workspace—couldn't have that.

His office was a perfectly fine place to spend his days. And some nights.

Okay, a lot of nights. And a lot of hours. Chris did what was needed to get the job done. His job was his life, and that was how he liked it.

The ugly paneled walls from the 1980s were mostly covered by bookshelves that held Chris's various diplomas and certificates, his law and reference books, a stash of John D. McDonald mysteries hidden in one corner, and several outdated textbooks. There were a few photographs—mostly work-related group shots from mind-numbing conferences. One was a snapshot of Chris with Ivan Morrison after Morrison's team had won trivia night a couple of years ago. Chris was sort of smiling, and Morrison's mouth was open in mid-laugh. Dante Castone had taken the picture because it was, he said, "Evidence that Chris Hatch actually leaves his cave once in a while."

So maybe McBride had a point. Dante'd had the photo printed and framed, then gave it to Chris for his birthday as a joke. Chris scowled at the image.

Castone was a sore spot for him at the moment. He'd get over it. Mostly, he felt like a fool for pining after a man who was clearly in love with someone else and had been for some time.

"Three weeks," McBride continued. God, he was a human steamroller Chris could do nothing to stop. "I've cleared your schedule. Paulter is covering in your absence."

Chris slammed his eyes shut. The trouble an unsupervised Ivan Morrison could get into in three weeks was... unfathomable. And now Agent Paulter was going to be the agent in charge? Chris wondered if the DEA's northwest regional offices would survive.

"Paulter? Did I hear you correctly?" Chris repeated. What the fuck was he going to do for three weeks away from his work—besides try and figure out how to surreptitiously keep Morrison and Paulter from ever being in the same room.

Fuck that, they couldn't be in the same building.

"Dennis Paulter will do a fine job. Go visit your family, Chris. I know you have one. Or climb a mountain or something."

"Paulter is a fool."

The man had been involved in more than one fucked-up op and yet somehow was still employed by the DEA. Chris had counted himself lucky never to have to deal with him directly. Until now. He wasn't sure whether the idea of Paulter *in charge* of Ivan Morrison made him want to laugh or cry.

"He is perfectly qualified to step in for you," McBride continued ruthlessly.

Chris loathed Dennis Paulter. Aside from being a shitty teammate, he was an ass-kissing know-it-all. The younger agent had been after his job for years. Chris was locking his desk drawers and taking the keys with him. He briefly wondered if there was a way to booby-trap his drawers.

"For fuck's sake," he said to his empty office. "What the hell am I going to do for three weeks?"

Fifteen days, not including the weekends. Chris had no life outside of his job. So-called work-life balance was a foreign concept to him. He was boring and he accepted it. But he was one hundred percent dedicated to his job, so if breaking up drug and sex trafficking rings meant he was boring? So be it.

"I don't know, but if I hear of you coming around the office, there will be disciplinary action," McBride said before ending the call.

Chris stared down at the cell phone he held in his hand and wondered if he'd imagined the entire conversation.

"Vacation? Just like that?"

Glancing up, he caught sight of the personalized Chris Hatch Pop Figure that Morrison had given him for some ridiculous reason—National Boss's Day, maybe. It acted as a sentry on his bookshelf and seemed to watch him from all directions. The head appeared to nod, mocking his question. The figurine even had a red cape, which Morrison had been particularly proud of.

No, dammit, he hadn't imagined the call. McBride was forcing him to take a break.

The damn phone rang again before he could set it aside—or

chuck it against one of the walls. Chris didn't normally resort to violence, but he was feeling the need for it today.

Without checking who was calling, he pressed Accept.

"Agent Hatch."

"Chris, honey! I'm so shocked I don't have to leave a voicemail!"

His mother sounded so happy he'd answered the phone that he felt a bit guilty for not calling recently.

"Hi, Mom."

But inwardly Chris groaned. He loved his parents, he truly did. They supported him in everything he did. When he'd come out to them in high school, Mom had given him a huge hug and Dad had too. They supported his career—for the most part. While Chris pretended he didn't know his dad smoked pot on a regular basis, at least it was legal in most places now.

Like all good parents, they just wanted him to be happy.

"You sound down, honey. What's going on? Is there a big case?"

"No," Chris answered honestly. "I'm being forced to go on vacation. For three weeks."

Once the words came out of his mouth, he cringed and squeezed his eyes shut again, immediately wishing he could take them back. If he'd been thinking clearly, he never would have said anything about the time off. His mom would insist he come for a visit, to Arizona where they'd retired a few years ago. Then again, it wasn't as if he had anywhere else to go.

"Vacation?!" His mom repeated with delight. "And three weeks, too? Come down here and visit us so we can fuss over you. It's been too long. One of our neighbors is traveling for the month, so you could do him a favor and house-sit. That way you could have some privacy."

"I don't know—" he began.

His mom cut him off. "Christopher Anthony Hatch, none of

us are getting any younger. Including you. Live a little. What are you going to do in Portland? Hole up in your house for three weeks?"

And so what if he just holed up? That actually sounded all right. What was wrong with hiding out, his only human contact being the pizza delivery person?

Unsurprisingly, by the time he'd gotten off the phone, Chris had agreed to spend his vacation time in Arizona at his parents' fifty-and-over community. Although he knew most of the residents were over sixty-five. Yippie-ki-yay.

Boy, didn't that sound thrilling. Better than a case of shingles, he supposed.

"You're our guest, so the fact that you're not quite fifty yet doesn't matter," his mom had assured him. Damn, it was almost as if his mom read his mind.

By the time they'd clicked off, Chris had also agreed to house-sit for Frank, the next-door neighbor. Susie Hatch's superpower was convincing people to do things she wanted them to without them realizing it. These days, Chris was onto her tactics, but he was almost as powerless against them as he'd been when he was a teen. She really should have been a politician.

"For fuck's sake, what was I thinking?" Leaning back in his chair, he allowed himself to release a groan that echoed around his office.

Truthfully, he'd had no real choice once his mom got started.

Truthfully, sitting at home for three weeks didn't appeal that much.

Chris had no hobbies outside of work. The pizza delivery guy was too young for him even in an imaginary porn flick, and he hated watching TV. The office was where he liked to be, in the eye of the hurricane.

Toeing the carpet, Chris spun his chair around in a slow circle.

Recently, that hurricane included Ivan Morrison. With Dante Castone permanently off the team, Morrison wasn't in the field as often as he had been. These days, he was invariably underfoot for reasons Chris couldn't begin to fathom. Morrison constantly turned up, claiming he had work to do that could only be taken care of at the office. Not long ago, he'd even cut his unruly hair, although it still wasn't quite regulation. And more unsettling, Chris wasn't sure he approved of the new style—he'd kind of liked the wild Morrison look.

The front office staff adored Ivan. More than once, Chris had had to yell through his office door, "Keep it down out there," like he was some sort of playground monitor.

Morrison was a damn good agent though. He played the fool, much to the bad guy's dismay but also something that often drove Chris up the wall. However, Chris couldn't complain too much when the bad guys kept falling for it.

Chris hadn't minded when Morrison started showing up around the office since it meant the agent hadn't been assigned to another undercover assignment. He would be soon though. Morrison was an excellent agent. But he couldn't help thinking that, if McBride thought Chris needed three weeks off, Morrison was definitely due for at least three months.

Chris stopped the chair for a second and reconsidered Morrison's increased visits. Was Morrison checking in, possibly worried Chris was upset that Dante had chosen Andre and not him? There were few personal secrets in an office the size of theirs. Chris had been distressed—at first. But ultimately, it didn't matter. He didn't have time for a relationship, and he'd never had a chance with Dante anyway.

Maybe, a little voice in his head had whispered when the dust settled, *you wanted him because you knew he'd never be yours.* Which was a truth that still stung more than anything else he'd considered.

Okay, that did it. Time to stop thinking and start planning the next few weeks.

One thing Chris did know was that he would miss Morrison's antics while he was away—his face peeking around Chris's office door, eyebrows waggling, his voice booming down the hallway as he finished telling the receptionist a joke.

How Morrison had gotten into undercover work in the first place, Chris couldn't begin to imagine. The man was not subtle.

Pushing against the carpet again, he spun himself in the other direction. He knew he should have left already. McBride's local spies were probably already clamoring to tell him that Chris was still in the building.

Fine. It would be fine. Everything would be fine.

The phone rang yet again. Chris eyed it and checked the screen this time. With a sigh, he clicked Accept.

"When I said today and now, I meant *today* and I meant *now*," McBride barked, then clicked off without letting Chris respond.

"Fucking hell."

With a sigh and a scowl, Chris rose to his feet and shrugged into the raincoat hanging on the back of his chair. Defiantly, he grabbed his laptop and shoved it into his briefcase, then snapped the case shut. If McBride thought Chris was leaving that item behind for Paulter to even sneak a glance at, he was sorely mistaken.

After one final quick look around, Chris released another sigh and headed out into the corridor. He grimaced at the newest front desk person as he passed by. Chris hadn't had time yet to learn their name, but they responded in turn with a tentative smile, so most likely he hadn't looked too threatening. It was lunchtime and no one else seemed to be in. Probably they'd all been given the heads-up by McBride.

Cowards.

TWENTY-FOUR HOURS LATER, Christopher Anthony Hatch, the man who never took a day off—no sick time, no personal time of any sort—found himself knocking on the front door of his parents' modular home in Surprise, Arizona.

"Christopher!" his mom exclaimed, a huge smile on her face, almost as if she was surprised he'd actually shown up. "It's so good to see you. Get yourself in here so I can give you a hug!" His mom grabbed the front of his hoodie in a tight grip. "Lance, get rid of the evidence, your son is here!"

Rolling his eyes, Chris allowed himself to be dragged over the threshold and tried not to groan too.

It was going to be a long three weeks.

TWO

Hatch

Chris's phone buzzed, pulling him away from the thriller he'd borrowed from his dad's bookshelf. Grateful for the interruption to the outrageous plot line, he set the paperback face down on the pavement beside the lounger he'd claimed earlier. Having learned from his most recent mistake, he checked the screen before answering, even though he suspected he knew exactly who was texting him this time.

He'd left Portland on Thursday, and the fact that he hadn't heard from Morrison until now was almost shocking. The man often called or texted him weekly, and it had been more often since Dante officially left town. Well, Chris mused, the two of them were close friends. Morrison probably missed Dante's company.

Something he refused to put a name to roiled in Chris's gut. Ignoring it, he scanned Morrison's text.

M: What the fuck? Where are you? Are you sick? Did you get fired?

Shaking his head and sighing, Chris waited a moment

before replying. Morrison could never just text everything he had to say in one go. Usually, it was a minimum of three texts before Chris responded.

M: Never mind. You didn't get fired. No way. No secret police types have stormed the building to remove your belongings.

Chris felt a smile curve his lips. Ivan Morrison was nothing if not always entertaining. And reliable. And damn smart.

M: Although… it is always the quiet ones who end up being the most surprising.

Smirking, Chris typed, **I wasn't fired. I'm in Arizona.** And then he waited for his phone to ring. Within seconds, the device vibrated in his hand.

"What the fuck? What are you doing in *Arizona?*" Morrison demanded, somehow making Arizona sound like it was the Amazon rainforest, or maybe Mars.

"HR decided I had to use my vacation hours. McBride said it was nonnegotiable."

"But… Arizona." Morrison's voice rose in disgust on the last letter of the state name. He sounded so outraged that Chris almost laughed.

"My folks live here now, moved down a few years ago. My mom happened to call right after McBride gave me the ultimatum. She caught me at a weak moment, I guess, suggested a visit, and I agreed." Chris released a sigh. "I enjoy my folks, and they even found somewhere for me to stay so I'm not underfoot at their place."

The last thing he needed was confirmation that his folks still had a sex life. Chris shuddered. He was bored though. He'd been on vacation for less than three days and was already going stir-crazy. How the hell did people actually retire?

"But you're bored."

Yep, smart.

"I've been here for three days, and I want to chew my own arm off. I've seen about all the mostly naked octogenarians that I can handle for one lifetime. For a fifty-and-over community, there's a surprising lack of fifty-year-olds. And I don't play golf. It's possible that I'm a little bored," he admitted.

Chris felt bad defaming the residents but honestly, there was a time and a place for naked, and it wasn't when you were pushing eighty-five. When he'd said something to this effect, his dad had called him a prude—but nicely.

"So, you're at some kind of nudist retirement community?" Morrison asked.

"I'm sure it's not official policy," Chris said dryly, glancing around at the occupants of the loungers spaced out on the grass in the common areas between modular homes, RVs, and the Olympic-sized swimming pool.

If residents weren't sunning themselves or swimming, they were playing golf. Some still worked as far as he could tell, but every morning so far, there'd been a line of folks waiting to get into the clubhouse at five thirty a.m. And all the residents appeared to own a golf cart, even his parents. Just how much golf could a person play? Admittedly, there were also painting and drawing opportunities, yoga classes, Pilates, and various book clubs.

Hobbies. He had to stifle a yawn just thinking about them.

What he needed was a good mystery to investigate. Something interesting to sink his teeth into. He could be his generation's Hercule Poirot. Maybe he needed one of those mystery-in-a-box games. Shutting his eyes, he suppressed a shudder.

"Are you near the Grand Canyon?" Morrison asked. "Are you going there? I've never been."

Chris opened his eyes again. "I am nowhere near the Grand Canyon. I wish. Instead, I'm at seven-fourteen Sunrise Surprise West in, you guessed it, Surprise, Arizona."

"How long are you gone for?"

"Around three weeks." Another twenty or so days and a few hours in change after HR had their say. But who was counting? Him. He was counting.

Chris's words were all but swallowed by the low rumble and roar of several motorcycles heading past where he was hanging out and on up Roadrunner Lane. He watched as they slowed down and turned into the driveway of a house across the street and slightly around the corner from his parents'. Chris could only see it now because of where he was sitting on Frank-the-Neighbor's tiny patio.

Two of the motorcycles were the three-wheeled trike kind. Five older dudes and one older gal, all of them in leathers, dismounted. They all stretched and rolled their necks before heading for the front door. Chris noted that between them, they had enough exposed tattoos to finance a small country. The lead biker raised his hand and knocked. He couldn't hear the banging from where he was sitting, but the man had a determined expression on his face. All of them did.

"I should have driven down, but I stupidly decided to fly," Chris added morosely. What had he been thinking? He was trapped in senior citizen hell. The aging motorcycle gang was the most interesting thing he'd experienced so far.

Here he was, soaking up the sunshine most Pacific Northwesterners craved at this time of year. Appropriately dressed in cargo shorts and a t-shirt, slathered in sunscreen, blinding people with his white legs—and all he was doing was feeling sorry for himself.

Across from Chris, the neighbor's door remained stubbornly closed. The woman stepped to the side of the stairs and tried to peek through the window. She must not have been able to see anything because she just shook her head and started back toward the bikes.

"I suppose I could rent a car for a day trip to the canyon. Dad says it's about three and a half hours from here. If I do, I'll send you some pictures."

"It's not as good as seeing it in person." Chris heard a shuffling sound he couldn't figure out. "Fucking Dennis Paulter is a tool. Why did he have to be the guy McBride put in your place? I should just put in for a real transfer to the feds, fuck this 'being loaned out' shit again."

Chris slowly shut his eyes for the briefest of moments. They cooperated with the local FBI office on a regular basis, but why was Morrison being sent there now? Was Paulter making important staff decisions while Chris was away? The highlight of most days was Morrison bursting into his office, and Paulter better not do anything to upset that. Ivan always arrived with some new bit of trivia or department gossip that hadn't made its way up to him or with the spiciest Sichuan tofu or phad Thai Chris had ever tasted.

And a goofy smile that Chris refused to find endearing.

"Do what he says, Morrison. Paulter doesn't have the kind of patience I do."

"And no sense of humor *whatsoever*. Right now, I'm cooling my heels, waiting on Radisson, the ultimate asshole."

Chris ignored the sense of humor comment. He didn't need to know what Morrison had been up to. Instead, he said, "Radisson's not that bad. Give him a chance."

Andy Radisson was the FBI agent in charge that Chris's people worked with most often, when investigations warranted it. He was a nice guy, and Chris actually liked him. And his team could be a good fit for Ivan and keep him off Paulter's radar. Chris made a mental note to reach out to Andy and give him the rundown on Morrison. With any luck at all, he could keep Ivan from going off the rails.

"Traffic getting here today was a fucking monster,"

Morrison complained. "Burnside was backed up going both directions, and some asshole almost rear-ended Big Blue."

"Heaven forbid," Chris said dryly.

Big Blue, a Ford Taurus sedan of indeterminate age, was Morrison's prized possession. It looked like a beater but was actually a James Bond-style decoy, complete with secret compartments, and easily reached one hundred and twenty miles an hour.

A sleeper, just like Morrison.

Chris refused to ask what Morrison had done to incur Paulter's ire. Because there was definitely a reason he was being loaned to the feds and they both knew it. And it had only been three official work days since he'd left.

"I've gotta go," Morrison said. "Looks like Radisson is ready to see me."

"Goodbye, Morrison. Try not to get into any more trouble while I'm gone."

Morrison mumbled something he didn't quite get followed by a, "Yeah, alright."

Setting the phone down in his lap, Chris leaned back in the lounger again so that the umbrella cast a shadow on his face. The thriller waited for him, but he wasn't interested in picking it back up.

Instead, he watched the senior citizen motorcycle gang stomp back to the street, mount their bikes, and ride off, clouds of dust billowing out behind them. Whatever they'd wanted, they were pissed the resident hadn't answered the door.

A rogue gust of wind chose that moment to whip up and blow a mix of sand and grit across the road in a whirlwind directly toward him. The thin coat of grime plastered his front and stuck to the sunscreen he'd applied earlier.

"Motherfucker."

This was officially the vacation from hell.

THREE

Morrison

"*Seven-fourteen Sunrise Surprise West, Surprise, Arizona,*" Ivan muttered to himself. "Well, that's a fuckton of surprises."

Ivan Morrison peered out of Big Blue's windshield to scan the numbers tacked up next to the house doors or on utility poles where there were RVs parked instead of modular homes.

"Seven-ten, seven-twelve..." he read aloud. "Ah, there it is, seven-fourteen, the magic number." Rolling to a stop, he set the parking brake and stared out the driver's side window. There it was, Hatch's forced vacation home.

"Not bad, not bad at all."

Admittedly, it had to be torture for Hatch not to be hard at work behind his desk. There was only one other time Hatch unexpectedly hadn't been in his office—that Morrison was aware of, at least. That time, Morrison had tracked him down at his home, where he'd been holed up with the flu and miserable as fuck—and still click-clacking away on his laptop. Luckily, the neighborhood phô place agreed to deliver several gallons of five-alarm broth, and Hatch had been back at his desk by the following Monday.

Seven-fourteen was a well-kept single-wide mobile home that had mutant orange lava rocks substituting for a lawn and bright terracotta pots with prickly pear and other cacti planted in them. Where the yard met the street were several healthy-looking aloe and century plants and—

He squinted at the yard art. Was that small statue a masturbating frog? Somebody in the house had a sense of humor.

Morrison sniggered. Everything he'd seen so far in Surprise was much too cheerful for Agent Christopher Hatch; the man tended to brood. Additionally, he chose only the deepest of blacks for his wardrobe most of the time—black suit, black tie. Add the black mood and voilà, Special Agent Hatch. It had to be hard for him to be gloomy when the sun was shining like it was today.

Yes, Morrison tended to wear black too, but that was because it hid the coffee stains. He was looking forward to lounging around in a t-shirt and shorts and getting some full-on vitamin D. He ran his fingers through his hair, still a little shocked at the current short haircut. It would grow back, he reminded himself.

The various lots in Sunrise had been developed along a semi serpentine-shaped road so they weren't right next to or directly across from each other—almost like an artist's rendering of the sun's rays. He'd spotted a clubhouse and Olympic-sized pool near the entrance. Common areas at one end of each street were littered with white plastic loungers, and at this time of day, not many were occupied, but a few dedicated citizens appeared to be actually enjoying the March heat.

"You did good, Blue." Morrison patted the dashboard of his car, a matte black souped-up sedan that no one suspected was owned by a law enforcement officer. And also, it was definitely not blue. Maybe didn't get the greatest gas mileage, but he cared more about being able to catch bad guys.

Almost as soon as he'd gotten off the phone with Hatch, he'd told Radisson he had a family emergency and didn't know when he'd be back. Radisson had tried to tell him to call Paulter instead, saying, "He's the man in charge right now," but Morrison had steamrolled right over that idea. He'd never liked Dennis Paulter much, and he certainly wasn't going to start acting like the man was his boss.

Nope. Not gonna happen. Radisson would do just fine. And it wasn't as if the FBI hadn't tried to recruit Morrison on a regular basis; Morrison was more than happy to do the shift in his mind now. Besides, regardless of what he'd said to Hatch on the phone, Morrison respected Agent Radisson and his team.

Radisson had conceded, which, Morrison found, many people eventually did when it came to something he really wanted. Probably, it was easier to deny his requests when he wasn't standing in front of them. But Morrison had been there for real and in person and not taking no for an answer. Besides, it turned out there was no case to work on; Paulter had just been offloading him.

After what turned out to be a pretty productive conversation, he'd headed back home much faster than the drive in, packed Blue, and hit the road.

Now, here he was in Arizona, the Grand Canyon State, and parked in front of Hatch's temporary house.

What had he been thinking coming down here uninvited?

Yes, he was generally impulsive and one hundred percent an adrenaline junkie, but as he'd aged—*like a fine fucking wine, thank you very much*—he'd learned to... moderate his impulses. At least that's what he told himself.

Anyway. What he'd been thinking was that Hatch had sounded depressed when he'd talked to him. And that Ivan didn't like not being able to just Kramer into Hatch's office when he wanted to and make him smile against his better judgment.

And he didn't like that Hatch was alone.

In general, there was a lot he didn't like about the current situation.

Sure, his parents lived around here somewhere. They'd invited their son to visit, after all. But what kind of people were they, really? In Morrison's experience, bio family was just not all that. There were no guarantees. And over the years they'd worked together, Chris Hatch had become a sort of family to Morrison—even if Hatch had no idea. Even if Hatch had been fixated on Dante Castone. So here he was in Arizona, making sure Hatch was okay.

That's what he'd told himself for twelve hundred plus miles, and that's the story he was sticking with.

Not that he felt brotherly toward Chris Hatch. Nope, not at all.

A tap against the passenger-side window had the combined benefit of bringing him back to reality and scaring the living shit out of him.

Whipping his head around, he expected to see Hatch, but instead of his boss—who was decidedly not his boss at the moment—it was an older woman. She had a shock of thick gray hair and wore a bright tie-dye shirt with a Grateful Dead skull on the front. Probably harmless.

He rolled the window down.

"Um, can I help you?" he asked.

"Are you lost? It can get kind of confusing around here."

The woman had kind eyes, a hazel brown that seemed familiar, and a kind smile too. He recognized that as well. Not that Hatch smiled a lot.

"I'm visiting my boyfriend." No way was he saying boss to

the woman he suspected was Hatch's mother, even if it technically wasn't currently true. The likeness was too close for them not to be related, though, and Morrison was an expert on Chris Hatch.

Expert sounded so much better than stalker. And boyfriend sounded better than scary boss-stalker dude. Yes, he nodded to himself, *boyfriend* covered just about everything in a non-creepy way.

Less creepy anyway.

"Chris said he was staying here on vacation. It's kind of a surprise, but I was in the area." If being in Portland, Oregon, one day and Arizona the next was *being in the area*. And once the words *boy* and *friend* had crossed his lips, he couldn't take them back.

What the actual fuck?

Morrison, goddammit, Hatch is going to kill you.

The woman's eyes widened, and a broad smile crossed her face.

"Christopher is my son!" she exclaimed. "He's with his dad checking out the Yuma Swap Meet. I don't know when they'll be back though, it's a few hours anyway."

She motioned for him to get out of the car. "Come over to our place while you wait for him. We can visit," she said with a great deal of excitement. "Would you like some iced tea or fresh lemonade? My name is Susie, by the way. Chris has never brought a boyfriend down here before. We've been so worried he was lonely back in Portland all by himself."

Morrison was very impressed; he couldn't have gotten a word in edgewise if he'd wanted to.

Susie Hatch moved purposefully around to the front of Blue, clearly expecting him to join her. Morrison noted the Grateful Dead shirt had the lightning-bolt skull on the back as well. A true Deadhead. He loved her already. Too bad he and

Hatch weren't really boyfriends, he'd definitely keep her for a mom.

Maybe he'd keep her anyway.

"I wouldn't say no to some lemonade," Morrison responded, smiling as he popped open the driver's side door and extricated himself from Blue. "My name's Ivan Morrison, by the way."

She stuck out her hand. "Chris is so quiet about his life. Fair warning, I plan on interrogating you. I want to hear everything. Let's be best friends before they get back," she said mischievously. "Expect to be plied with lemonade and cookies."

Morrison's grin widened. Two could play this game, and Hatch wasn't here to stop him or Hatch's mother. He'd deal with the fallout later.

"I love cookies. I think we're going to get along just fine," he agreed, locking the car and following Susie to the front door of seven-sixteen. "I can't imagine why Hatch hasn't introduced us before now."

SEVERAL HOURS LATER, Ivan and "Call me Susie" were comfortably ensconced on the Hatches' backyard patio, chatting like they'd known each other forever. Morrison was on his third lemonade but only the first with alcohol—mostly alcohol if he was being honest.

But he wasn't driving, was he? No, he was flipping through a photo album dedicated to Christopher Hatch as a teenager. There were several of them; he'd already been through Chris Hatch, the Early Years.

Hatch *was* going to kill him and Morrison didn't care one iota. It wasn't as if he'd begged Susie to break out the photo albums. She'd gone inside to refill the pitcher of lemonade— "Adding a little vodka this time!"—and brought them back outside with her.

Leaning closer, he peered at High School Hatch, who'd been on the debate team as well as track. Past Christopher Hatch seemed to be just as moody as current-day Hatch. Morrison wanted to travel back in time and give him a much-needed hug.

He flipped the page, and another, and another.

Toward the end of that album was a snapshot of Hatch with his parents. They stood on either side of him, their arms wrapped around his shoulders and huge smiles on their faces—Susie and Lance's faces, at least. Chris was scowling and decked out in black jeans, a black sweater, and black shoes. His parents, on the other hand, were dressed in blindingly colorful tie-dye, one in a shirt that said Whirled Peas on the front and the other in one emblazoned with Grateful Peace. Susie also had on a bright purple skirt while Lance sported baggy cargo shorts. They both wore Birkenstocks. With socks.

It was the most beautiful thing he'd ever seen.

"Did you and Lance"—he hadn't met the man yet and they were already on a first-name basis too—"purposefully torture Chris by wearing cheerful clothing?"

"Oh." Susie giggled. "Sort of? Okay, yes. I can't lie. Don't tell him though. We've never admitted it to him. He's just always so serious, and we have a bad habit of trying to make him laugh."

"Does it work?"

"Sometimes," she admitted. "Not as often as we'd like. He's a good boy though."

Morrison liked to make Hatch laugh too. It didn't happen nearly often enough.

He started to say something, but the rumble and roar of many motorcycles drowned him out. The noise was so deafening and close that it could only be coming from the street directly out front. Susie rolled her eyes.

"Those people," was what Morrison thought she said.

It was too loud for conversation. Then the roaring ended abruptly, and the silence that followed was a relief.

"That might be Ray Walker and his"—she used air quotes—"motorcycle club. Ray and his friends are more annoying than anything. But." She shook her head in a *what can you do* kind of way.

Morrison felt there might be a story he needed to know. "But what?"

Susie rolled her eyes. "Now you really sound like Chris. But nothing. Ray is just an old man who always wanted to be a tough guy. When he retired, he bought himself a badass motorcycle, gathered up a few friends, and now they ride together. Their motto is Ride or Die, which I find hilarious and ironic seeing as everyone living here is closer to death than we'd like. They're all over seventy, and they're going to die sooner rather than later."

She laughed and Morrison laughed along with her, but he also made a mental note to ask Chris what his opinion was regardless of the riders' ages. Not all MCs dabbled in the illegal unless you counted speeding—and Morrison could totally understand the need for speed—but being an *almost-former* DEA agent meant he'd been involved in more cases involving illegal MCs than he could count on two hands. A nervous shiver rolled down his spine.

"More lemonade?" Susie asked. "It's happy hour after all, and we have plenty of vodka."

"Don't mind if I do," Morrison said agreeably.

FOUR

Chris squinted through his dad's windshield, not sure he believed what his eyes were seeing, but regardless how many times he blinked, they kept telling him the same thing.

A matte black Ford Taurus was parked in front of Frank's place. What were the chances that his parents' friend—or anyone else in their lives down here—owned a car that looked exactly like Ivan Morrison's?

And had Oregon plates?

None.

He asked the question anyway. "Dad, what kind of car does Frank own?"

"Oh, um." His dad flicked the turn indicator and maneuvered into the narrow parking space next to their home. "Frank has a RAV4, I think, and a motorbike. Why? Are you thinking about buying a car? We could check out a few while you're down here."

The only thing worse than spending the day wandering around the swap meet would be wandering around several used car lots. He'd still be hot and sweaty, but he'd also have to fend off smarmy salesmen.

"No, Dad, I am not in the market for a new car at the moment."

A sinking-tingly feeling of dread plus anticipation made his stomach churn. There was only one person in the world that the ugliest car Chris had ever laid eyes on belonged to, and that was Ivan Morrison.

Ivan Morrison, whose picture should be next to the word *chaos* in Webster's Dictionary: Ivan Morrison, Chaos Factor.

What the hell was Ivan Morrison doing in Surprise, Arizona?

There was only one way for him to find out. Chris pushed open the car door but paused with one foot on the pavement and one still inside the car as a more horrifying thought occurred to him. Frank's house was locked up tight right now.

Where exactly was Ivan Morrison, and just how long had he been here?

"Sounds like your mom has guests over," his dad commented innocently over his shoulder, turning away from the front door and instead heading around to the back patio.

"Guest, one guest," Chris corrected as he scrambled to get out of the car. "What the actual fuck?"

"What? Is something the matter?" Lance asked.

Everything was the matter. Morrison and his parents, together? Disaster.

Jogging across the street, Chris swiped his hand across the hood of the Taurus. It had been parked in the shade of a palm tree and was cool to the touch—at least, not scorching hot. He tried to calculate how just long that would take and thus how many hours Morrison had been there, and... he couldn't. The answer was *too long.*

"Nothing, just... nothing," Chris said, catching back up with his dad.

After an entire day wandering the swap meet with Lance Hatch, all Chris wanted to do now was hide over at Frank's place with a cold beer and maybe some cheap Mexican food. The dream slipped from his grasp when a deep, loud laugh that he recognized as Ivan Morrison's reached his ears. He'd heard it often enough, after all. And as much as it irritated him in the moment, the sound inevitably made him smile in other circumstances. Morrison always made him smile.

He wasn't smiling now. No way. Not going to happen.

His dad looked over his shoulder again, motioning for him to hurry up. "Come on, son, sounds like happy hour has already started."

Chris slowly trailed after his dad while still trying—and failing—to work out what the fuck Morrison was doing in Arizona.

It couldn't be anything good.

COMING around the corner of the house, Chris paused and watched his dad kiss his mom on the head and then plop down on the chair next to hers.

As he'd thought, it was only Morrison and his mom out on the patio. The neighbors hadn't been invited over for an impromptu party—not yet anyway. But the two of them had been making enough noise to wake the dead. Luckily, quiet hours didn't start for a while.

His mom appeared to notice Chris first. *Appeared* being the operative word. Morrison wouldn't still be alive if he wasn't always aware of his surroundings. Even if the empty tumbler in his large hand indicated the man had finished off at least one of his mom's dangerous "special" vodka lemonades.

"Sweetheart!" his mom exclaimed. "Look who I found!"

Morrison shot him a cheeky grin and Chris narrowed his eyes at him in return. Morrison shrugged back.

Oh, yeah, the man knew he was in deep shit.

"Dad, this is"—Chris scrambled for the right words—"my friend, Ivan Morrison. Morrison, this is my dad, Lance. I see you've met Mom already."

"Don't be afraid to use the word boyfriend, Chris," his mom gushed. "We've been chatting for hours. I can't believe you've never mentioned Ivan to us before. But he explained that you've only recently decided you two are serious. Makes my mom heart so happy." His mom clapped one hand across her chest dramatically and nowhere near her heart. Chris speculated that Susie's lemonade specials must be even stronger than usual, and they were usually damn strong.

Now Morrison was decidedly not looking Chris's way. Chris moved over, directly into Morrison's line of sight, and mouthed, *Boyfriend?*

Morrison shrugged again. Chris decided to ignore the fact that he wasn't exactly pissed off by Morrison's use of the word.

"I'm so happy to have a chance to use this new glassware," his mom continued, oblivious to the half-hearted death glare Morrison was receiving. "And I just made a fresh pitcher of lemonade and was about to pour Ivan another. Let's celebrate!"

She held her hand out for Morrison's tumbler. He gave it to her without hesitation and damn if Susie didn't fill it to the rim. A tray with two more empty glasses sat on a low table by her elbow. It was going to be a long night.

"Have a seat, honey." Deftly, his mom poured her concoction into each glass and handed one to his dad and the other to Chris.

Accepting the drink, Chris surveyed the scene of the crime. He caught Morrison's eye again and raised one eyebrow with an added *what the fuck* cock of his head. Morrison shot back yet another expressive single-shoulder shrug. So many shrugs and not one of them was a guilty one.

That was the moment Chris spotted the photo albums sitting off to one side of Morrison's chair. Stepping past him, Chris snatched the top one and held it up for all to see.

"Photo albums?" He shook the offending book and set it back down. "Really, Mom?" He infused his voice with the tone he usually reserved for employees who'd stepped over the line. Morrison had heard it plenty. And much like with Morrison, it had no effect on his mother.

"Now, don't get yourself all riled up," she said with a broad smile, handing the re-filled drink back to the uninvited guest. "Have a seat already." She leaned across and patted the empty patio chair next to Morrison. "I'm just so happy for the two of you. Lance, make a toast."

"IVAN TELLS me you two met at work," Mom said, her smile taking in the both of them.

"I suppose that's the truth," Chris allowed.

Chris sat in the open seat next to Morrison and sipped at his refreshed drink. He was going to kill Morrison later, but it also wasn't the worse thing in the world to let his folks think he had a real boyfriend, that he wasn't all work and no play—even though he so was. He eyed his half-empty glass; it was probably time to slow down.

"We met at the same office," Morrison agreed. "But I'm transferring to a different organization, and I ended up with some time off between assignments because of that."

He was transferring? Since when? He had time off? That actually wasn't a shock. But this was the first Chris had heard of a transfer. Wasn't he being loaned out? Had Morrison requested the transfer? Was the move permanent? What the fuck was going on in Portland while he was on vacation? He made a mental note to call Radisson and find out exactly what was happening. Paulter was useless for information.

"I'm a bit of a maverick," Morrison continued. Chris snorted, earning himself a look from Susie. "The current boss and I don't see eye to eye. Chris and I met at trivia night a while back. Opposite teams. Mine trounced his team, and I think I impressed him with my knowledge of the TV show, *MASH*."

They *had* met at that trivia night event, the one immortalized in the picture in his office, before Ivan ended up working directly for Chris. He'd forgotten that fact. And, yes, Ivan's team had won that night. But that's only because Chris had been forced to team up with some yahoo from accounting. And Dennis Paulter. Fucking Paulter.

"I had to team up with Paulter, you know that. Although for someone who wasn't born before *MASH* ended, you sure do know a lot about the show."

"And you were what, five?" Morrison shot back.

"And now you're moving in together," his mom interjected, all starry-eyed.

Chris inhaled sharply, choking and coughing on the swig of toxic lemonade he'd just taken. Morrison pounded him on the back.

"You alright?" Ivan asked him.

"Just," Chris rasped when he could speak, "lemonade— wrong way."

"Lance and I met at a Grateful Dead concert," Mom said, unfazed by Chris's coughing fit. "Remember, honey?"

"That's right," Dad concurred, scooting closer to his life partner and swinging his free arm over her shoulders. "It was love at first sight. They were playing *Uncle John's Band*, and Gerry was on guitar. It was hot and they had sprinklers running all around the venue, so there were rainbows everywhere. I'll never forget that day."

"We danced the rest of the night away. I think we were both high as kites on mushrooms."

"Mom," Chris said warningly.

"Oh, Chris, I just don't know sometimes. Always so serious. If you didn't look so much like me, I'd think you weren't our child. Well, that and the thirty-six hours of labor you put me through."

The reminder of the not-so-quite-in-the-past drug use—at least now, Chris hoped, his dad *just* smoked pot—was more than enough. And Chris did not need a play-by-play of the day he was born. He'd heard it enough times already.

"I think Chris takes after both of you," Morrison said, scooting his chair closer to Chris's and draping his arm across his shoulders, a mirror of what Lance had done.

Not for the first time since Ivan Morrison stormed into his life, Chris noted that he enjoyed the smell of Morrison's cologne. Maybe it was just Morrison's scent in general. The heavy weight of his arm was reassuring as well, keeping Chris from completely freaking out because his parents believed they were an item.

It wasn't the worst thing that could happen while he was on vacation, he reminded himself. If his parents thought he and Morrison were together, maybe they'd stop pestering him about "true love" and all that bullshit. Maybe his mom would stop worrying about him being alone for the rest of his life, as if having personal space was a death sentence.

"It must be hard worrying about each other. I know Chris isn't in the field as much as he once was, but still."

"We've seen a lot, you know," Morrison agreed. "A lot of bad stuff comes from drug running. Sh-stuff I wouldn't wish on my worst enemy."

Susie nodded. "I understand that. Just a couple of weeks ago, some locals were found locked up in a Conex box out in the desert. Police said it was a drug deal gone wrong. I can't even imagine."

Chris could imagine. He'd seen it with his own eyes. So had Morrison. Ivan squeezed his shoulder.

"I'm a bit peckish," Morrison said. "Is there a good place to eat around here?"

If he'd hoped to change the subject, food was an excellent choice. Chris figured he really was hungry though.

"It takes some serious calories to keep up this svelte figure." Ivan motioned to his chest.

Was Morrison self-conscious of his size? Yeah, the man was big, but it was mostly muscle. If he had a little extra, it suited him, and therefore it was not extra.

"We've got plenty to go around," his mom said. "Right, Lance?"

But first, his mom poured more drinks all around, and when those were empty, his dad fired up the barbecue. It was a damn good thing none of them were driving anywhere.

They laughed and talked loudly about nothing important while scarfing down Lance's world-famous barbecue chicken and seared corn on the cob. Chris hadn't laughed that hard or felt that comfortable around his parents in years. Maybe ever. And it was all because of Ivan, who fit like the perfect odd-shaped puzzle piece between Chris and his folks.

When everyone was finished eating, Chris and Morrison took everything inside and loaded the dishwasher before saying their goodbyes.

"Thanks for feeding us, Lance," Morrison declared while rubbing his stomach in satisfaction. "I haven't had a meal like that in ages."

"You're welcome, son. We'll do it again tomorrow night!"

FIVE

Morrison

"Oh, my god," Morrison groaned while Chris took his time unlocking the front door. "Hurry the fuck up, I have to pee."

"Serves you right," Chris said heartlessly, turning the key and pushing the door open. "Mom's drinks are always dangerous. It's best to pace yourself. How many did you have anyway?"

Morrison had no clue and couldn't calculate anything due to the aforementioned need to urinate. "You weren't here to warn me, so how was I supposed to know? And anyway, I was pacing myself. But then I lost count."

Chris stepped aside so Morrison could go ahead of him.

"Losing count is inevitable when Susie Hatch is making the drinks, and extremely dangerous."

"Where's the damn bathroom?" Ivan couldn't see well in the dim interior. Why didn't the owner at least have a couple of handy night-lights?

"Down the hall to the right. Watch the coffee table there."

Turning toward the hallway Chris had indicated, Morrison

immediately knocked into the coffee table. Pain radiated from his shin, almost but not quite overwhelming his need to use the bathroom.

"Fucking motherfucker, that hurt."

The coffee table hadn't budged from its spot in the middle of the carpet. It was a beast, with what appeared to be several sets of encyclopedias piled onto a shelf underneath while the upper surface was covered with magazines set in stacks, like the place was a hair salon or doctor's office.

Morrison heard Chris's distinct snort as he pulled the front door shut.

"Was that a laugh?" he asked. His eyes had adjusted to the gloom, and he began to move across the room more carefully. Who knew what else the owner had stashed in plain sight?

"Maybe it was."

Morrison made it into the bathroom without further injury and quickly took care of business. When he returned to the living room, a knock-off Tiffany-style lamp had been turned on and Chris was relaxed on a truly heinous couch Morrison had somehow missed on his first pass-through. Personally, he thought the couch was better served by the dark.

The thing should've been in a horror museum. The frame was made of wicker, maybe bamboo, and spray-painted black by an amateur who'd missed huge swatches of the thing. Some of the ugliest floral upholstery and matching pillows Morrison had ever seen hid the worst of the paint job, but not all of it. The piece of furniture took up most of the real estate against one wall, across from a picture window looking onto the street.

"Will that hold both of us?" he asked doubtfully.

Chris raised an eyebrow at him. "I guess there's only one way to find out."

"I could sit in the matching chair, I suppose." He took another good look at the couch and the equally weirdly spray-painted chair. "Who puts this kind of shit inside their house? Isn't this outdoor furniture?"

"We're in Arizona, Ivan. Life works differently here."

Ivan. Gah.

Morrison's heart stuttered. He loved hearing his first name roll off Chris's tongue the way it was meant to be spoken. How many times could he get Chris to say his given name while they were pretending to be boyfriends?

Admittedly, Ivan hadn't been kidding about the boyfriend thing. This forced vacation was a gift from the federal gods, his best chance to get Hatch to see him as someone *other* than the guy he needed to constantly monitor. As the man who loved Chris Hatch regardless of his Little Black Cloud tendencies. And anyway, most of the shit he got up to was just to get Chris's attention.

What could he say? That laser stare of Chris's turned him on.

With care, Ivan lowered his weight down onto one side of the couch. No way was he sitting in the chair. He wanted to be as close to Chris Hatch as possible. When Ivan Morrison made a plan, he stuck to it.

And if that sounded a bit creepy in his head, he didn't mean it that way. He was just glad he hadn't said anything out loud. Fingers crossed. Quickly, he glanced at Chris; nope, his ex-boss wasn't staring at him like he'd said something inappropriate.

Counting that as a win.

Shifting around, he made the couch creak under the additional weight, but it held. Exchanging a goofy grin with Chris, he settled back against the cushions and directed his gaze out the window, where he could see that the neighborhood was getting ready for the night. Lights were clicking on inside the homes, the blue flicker of TV sets was gleaming through front windows, and he heard something that sounded an awful lot like a car engine trying to start.

"What's that sound?" he asked.

Chris listened for a moment. "Cactus wren."

"That's a bird? No way."

"Yes, way."

Hatch was, possibly, as relaxed as Morrison had ever seen him. His arms were slung across the back of the couch and one ankle rested on the opposite knee. This was one of the first times he had seen Chris not wearing anything that wasn't a suit, suit-related, or suit-adjacent. Not the very first time, but no more than the fifth time for sure.

The first instance had been a year ago, when Special Agent in Charge Hatch had answered Ivan's knock on his front door wearing a pair of disheveled pajama bottoms and a hoodie with an unidentifiable stain on it. Human after all.

"You look good in shorts," Morrison blurted. "And the t-shirt is nice too." He refrained from commenting on the fact that they were all black.

Chris looked down at himself as if he'd forgotten what he was wearing.

Oh, damn. There went his mouth.

Glancing back up at him, Chris said, "So, I guess there are some things we need to talk about, *Boyfriend*."

Morrison grimaced and groaned, knowing what was coming next. His big mouth went and got him in trouble. Again. He wished he could blame the alcohol, but he wasn't drunk, just tipsy.

"No need to talk. Nope, nope, nope," he said, dragging his thumb and index finger across his lips as if zipping them together. "Zip it, lock it, put it in my pocket."

For a second Chris stared at him, eyebrows drawn together in what appeared to be utter confusion. Then, without warning, a bubble of laughter burst from him. This was followed by more, louder, hoots of laughter. And he kept laughing. Bemused, Morrison watched as Chris flung himself forward and wrapped his arms around his middle while he lost it, his shoulders shaking as he huffed and guffawed.

Chris Hatch. Mister Fucking Serious. Howling with laughter until tears were streaming down his face, and it was beautiful, joyous. Ivan wanted to make it happen over and over.

Doubt he'd been pushing aside reared its head and hammered into him.

This whole shenanigan was ridiculous. Of all the shenanigans he'd ever shenaniganned, this one... He paused his train of thought to ponder for a moment: Just how big was a shenanigan?

Anyway, moving right along.

It was beyond outrageous that he'd driven all the way to Arizona to barge in on Chris's vacation. There was no way anyone would ever believe Chris would be interested in him, much less want the label of Ivan Morrison's boyfriend. But laughter was the most infectious disease of them all, and regardless of his self-doubt, Morrison found himself laughing along with him.

Eventually, they laughed themselves out. The room turned quiet and Chris was watching him closely—probably wondering if Ivan had finally lost his last marble. Ivan quieted down, feeling twitchy under the piercing scrutiny.

"So, we're boyfriends, right?" Chris asked, wiping his eyes. "Just clarifying, getting the story straight, so to speak. And we're moving in together as soon as your lease is up?"

So, *not* wondering about Ivan's grasp on reality then. That was a relief.

"You know what happens, Chris." No way was he uttering the word boss at this moment. "A thought gets into my head and suddenly *boom*. Your mom surprised me, and it just popped out." And anyway, Chris wasn't his boss anymore, or almost wasn't, even if he didn't know it yet. He really needed to tell Chris he'd put in for a permanent transfer to Radisson's team.

"It just popped out," Chris repeated, snorting again. "Look, Ivan, I *know* you, not only as part of my team but also from reading your file. You've withstood interrogations by hardened motorcycle gang members. You've infiltrated gangs running drugs, weapons, and humans from Canada to Mexico. My mom is not that scary."

"Her lemonade is damn strong."

"I may be a little drunk right now," Chris continued. "Okay, a lot drunk. But I'm pretty damn sure that Mom's lemonade didn't make you say those things. Or sit there and flip through all seventeen of the photo albums she and Dad put together."

"Eighteen," Ivan corrected. "Susie said she just finished the last one this past winter. And, oh my god, that picture of you and your folks at your college graduation. I think that's my favorite."

"See?" Chris pointed a wobbly index finger in his direction. "That's what I'm talking about." His eyes narrowed thoughtfully. "You want to think there's something interesting in me— always dropping by the office, hanging out, sharing your five-alarm take-out, trying to *connect* or something. Which is"—he shrugged and flailed his hands—"ridiculous. I am the world's most boring person. Add to that the fact that I pined—*pined*— after someone for fucking years when I knew he wasn't inter-ested in me? Boring *and* an idiot. Go figure."

Wait. Ivan stopped breathing for a moment.

Chris thought *he* was boring? Was Morrison having an auditory hallucination?

"You're not boring," Ivan said seriously. "You're reliable.

Although you have to admit, the phad Thai from that food truck is amazing."

"Hmph." Skepticism oozed from the single word. "I'm reliable. So reliable that I racked up enough vacation to have myself literally forced by the higher-ups to take time off. And there was nowhere for me to go except my parents' fifty-and-up retirement community in Arizona. I have nothing better to do than work. 'Get a hobby,' they say. What the fuck should I do? Start needlework? Does a person just randomly wake up and decide, 'Today is the day I am going to start collecting rocks'?"

Morrison leaned over and kissed his boss.

On the lips.

SIX

Chris

Ivan's lips moved tentatively against his at first. The scruff of his beard was unfamiliar, but not unwelcome. When Chris didn't immediately pull away, Ivan pressed harder, his large hands lifting to frame Chris's face, holding him in place.

As if he was going anywhere.

Chris was shocked, but not the way he knew he should've been. He should've been stopping Ivan. Saying no. But he didn't want to and he wasn't going to. In fact, he wanted Ivan closer. Reaching around the bigger man's body, he tugged at Ivan's t-shirt until the man got the damn hint and swung one leg over Chris's lap so he was straddling him.

"We're gonna break this damn couch," Ivan murmured between gentle caresses.

"We'll buy what's-his-name a new one," Chris said, his voice rough.

"Frank," Ivan reminded him.

He'd never allowed himself to imagine Ivan as a lover; it was a line he'd not permitted himself cross. Or a line he'd even admitted existed between himself and Ivan. But somewhere buried inside, he'd known the attraction was there.

Even so, gentle Ivan was a surprise. Deep in his brain, Chris noted that it shouldn't have been so. He tucked that thought away to examine later. Maybe Ivan was worried Chris would shrink from his touch. Push him away. Order him out of the house. Chris thought he might shatter, but it wasn't going to be because Ivan's gentle hands were on him. It was going to be because he hadn't known how much he'd really wanted this.

Ivan Morrison, chaos factor. Gentle like lightning.

Ivan must have sensed his distraction. "Is this okay?" he asked, his tone laced with concern and possibly a dash of insecurity.

"Yes," Chris said firmly, trying to pull him closer so he could wrap his arms around him.

"You're *sure* sure?" Now it was Ivan who hesitated, pulling away to look Chris directly in the eye. "This isn't vodka induced, right?"

"No. And, yes, I'm sure. I know when my mom's drinks are influencing me—and this isn't one of those times."

Maybe the vodka had helped to lower the walls he'd built around himself, but he'd wanted Ivan for a while now. He just couldn't hide from that truth anymore.

"I've wanted this forever," Ivan whispered as he returned his attention to Chris's mouth.

He had? That was a discussion for later.

For now, Chris let himself be swept away by the tsunami of want and need barreling through him. The weight of Ivan kept Chris in place, pinned against the hideous fucking couch. Or maybe it was gravity doing its job, making sure Chris didn't float off into the ether.

Ivan's tongue darted against Chris's lips, asking permission for more. With quiet desperation, Chris opened his mouth and let him in.

He lost track of their surroundings, of time. He couldn't remember when he'd last just made out with a guy. Had he ever just let himself enjoy his partners? Sadly, Chris suspected the answer might be no. Wham-bam, don't let the door hit you on the ass, that had always been his preference. No strings meant no getting hurt.

Ivan wouldn't hurt him, Chris was confident of that. Would he hurt Ivan? Not on purpose. But he worried what they were doing would not have a happy ending, and Chris would end up making his parents sad. Again.

"Quit thinking so fucking hard, it's distracting me," Ivan complained, rocking against him.

They were both going to have beard burn in the morning but hey, in for a penny and all that.

"Should we take this into the bedroom?" Chris asked. He ran his hands down and across Ivan's strong back; the slight shiver he felt under his fingertips was the perfect reward.

Ivan pulled away and, as stifling as it was inside the house, Chris felt cold.

"Are you sure about that?" Ivan asked, worry in his eyes.

"I'm sure." Chris waggled his eyebrows, thrusting his hips upward. "Are you sure?"

"Damn right I'm sure." Ivan hopped up and off Chris's lap. "Where's the damn bedroom?"

With a laugh, Chris pointed down the hall, chuckling as he followed Ivan to the bedroom. Hopefully, Frank would never know Chris and Morrison had enjoyed sexy fun times in his bed.

Maybe this vacation was going to turn out all right after all.

Frank's dimly lit bedroom wasn't much, and the mattress certainly didn't compare to the one Chris had in Portland, but it would do. Ivan paused at the door, gesturing him inside with a goofy, "After you."

Resisting the temptation to push him up against the door frame just so he could experience Ivan's big body more thoroughly, Chris brushed past him into the room. Quickly, he divested himself of most of his clothing—all except his boxers—and climbed onto the bed.

"I'm not shy or unsure about this, but I didn't bring any supplies and it's been a hot minute since I've been tested," he told Ivan.

Ivan swaggered toward the bed. "I've passed my recent exams with flying colors, so, next time. After your physical." He waggled his eyebrows making Chris smile—again.

"Oh, there's going to be a next time?" Chris teased back.

Ivan halted with one knee up on the bed, pushing it down. "Hell, yes, there's going to be a next time." He sounded almost outraged. "It's taken me this long to get here, I'm not running the bases just once."

Chris patted the sheet. "Quit stalling."

"Stalling? I am wooing. I'm afraid if I move too fast, you might startle, come to your senses and disappear."

"Ivan," Chris said, earning a glance full of heat and promise. "I'm not going anywhere. Maybe I should take these off, after all." Deftly, he tugged the boxers off so he was completely naked and rolled onto his back so Ivan could see for himself that Chris didn't want him anywhere but in bed.

With him.

Ivan stared, seemingly speechless, watching as Chris pumped his own cock. He'd been half erect already so it didn't take any time at all for his cock to fill his fist. A little precome pulsed out his tip.

"Are you just going to stare, or are you going to do something about this?" A wordless Ivan was something of a novelty. Chris thrust his hips upwards a couple times, his grip on his cock tight and sending sparks of need up his spine.

Shaking his head, possibly because his brain was coming back online, Ivan tugged the last of his clothing off and got on the bed beside Chris. Scooting as close as was comfortable, he tugged at Chris's forearm.

"Lemme do that," he rumbled.

Relaxing his fist, Chris felt Ivan's fingers wrap around him and tentatively pump. Ivan was hard too. His bare cock brushed against Chris's thigh, making him wish he was the kind of guy who was always prepared.

"I like it hard and fast," he informed Ivan.

"That's good information. But I bet that's because you don't like to waste time, Mister Efficient. We're not doing this fast, Chris. Shift onto your side."

He moved as he'd been commanded and was tempted to say something about Ivan being bossy, but then Ivan dragged his thumb underneath his glans and Chris couldn't remember his name anyway. Almost by instinct, he wrapped the arm not trapped under his body around Ivan's neck and drew his head closer to him, claiming his mouth for himself.

Ivan released a deep groan. His lips parted and his moving hand faltered for a second before starting up again, sending fireworks of pleasure that cascaded through Chris's body. He was a river, a waterfall, a stream defrosting after a long, cold winter. Ivan was hot as the sun, relentlessly hot like a desert, brazenly hot like nuclear fusion. His entire purpose in this moment was to thaw Chris, to turn him into a pliable and needy being. And it was working.

Wresting back some of his fabled control, Chris plunged his tongue into Ivan's mouth. His partner tasted of spicy barbecue and lemonade at first, but that was quickly forgotten. Kissing was an art as far as Chris was concerned. If you couldn't take your time with it, why bother? And Ivan Morrison knew how to kiss. He didn't stiffen his lips, he melded them against Chris's. His tongue danced with Chris's, flicking and teasing.

It was fucking sexy.

Ivan's big hands and long fingers were wrapped almost entirely around both of their cocks—and through this *kissing*, he kept pumping. Chris didn't know which sensation to focus on, the silken glide of their erections catching against each other or the way Ivan's tongue dragged across Chris's lips before he gently bit down on them.

"Oh, fuck, *Ivan*."

His hips thrust convulsively. Chris was so close to coming, and from the heave of Ivan's chest, he was too. Shifting again, Ivan pulled away, to make just enough space between their bodies so he could take them both to the stars.

There was nothing except low ambient light illuminating the bedroom. Still, Chris peered down between their bodies, watching Ivan's hand piston slowly. Up, a squeeze, and down again. His balls tightened, the fireworks became conflagration. The show was about to reach its glorious end.

Ivan did one last sly twisty movement that sent Chris over the edge. His come pulsed out, spilling over Ivan's fingers and the sheet, his cock twitching with the effort to still empty when nothing was left. Seconds later, Ivan was coming too, throwing his head back, his body stiffened for a moment as he groaned long and loud.

They lay there for a while, the sound of their breathing filling the empty spaces in his heart. Chris shut his eyes and started to drift off, only waking when Ivan got up and quickly returned with a warm cloth to clean them up.

"Thanks. Next time it's my turn," Chris murmured as he began to drift off. Just before he fell completely under sleep's spell, he felt Ivan spoon up behind him and wrap his big arm around Chris's middle, pulling him close.

Chris smiled.

CHRIS WAS the warmest and most contented he'd been in way too long.

He didn't want to move, and the pillow over his face didn't even bother him. The first pop that had trespassed into his subconscious, he simply incorporated into his dream. He knew he wanted to ignore the sound.

But then there was a second distinct pop, followed by silence, and now Chris was fully awake.

"What the hell," he muttered.

"What the *fucking* hell?" Ivan responded dryly. "Not a car backfiring, that's for sure. Isn't this a retirement community?"

Sighing, Chris released his grip on the pillow and sat up.

"Retirement community doesn't mean no weapons allowed. I bet some of these folks have full arsenals. I was hoping it was just a dream."

"Sadly, no. Unless we're doing some weird magic and sharing the same dreams." Ivan rubbed the sleep from his eyes. "Although I suppose that could be possible," he said with a leer. "Sex magic is a thing, after all."

"Highly doubtful. Dammit. Last time I was down here the most exciting thing to happen was a near trampling when there wasn't enough food at the Sunday barbecue."

"It's not Sunday," Ivan pointed out.

"Nope."

"Well, fuckity fuck."

With a deeply felt grunt, Ivan sat up and rolled off the bed to his feet. For a second or so, he just stood there with his hands on his hips and a pout on his face. Then he spun around, waggled his ass at Chris, and grabbed yesterday's shorts and t-shirt up from the carpet.

Yawning, Chris swung his legs out from under the sheet and fumbled around in the gloom for his shorts and boxers. They were both dressed in seconds. For a big guy, Chris had always been surprised by how quickly Ivan moved. He was deceptively fast, intelligent, and damn sexy.

Why the hell had Chris ignored him for as long as he had? Probably because Chris had refused to recognize Ivan as more than an employee.

Well, shit.

That was going to be an issue. Maybe.

The growl of motorcycle engines roaring to life urged Chris to hurry the fuck up. Ivan had his shorts and a sleeveless t-shirt on first and bolted from the bedroom with Chris close behind. By the time they reached the front door and threw it open, the bikes were gone, the roar of their engines fading quickly as the vehicles raced away.

The neighborhood was eerily quiet. A few interior lights were on, but that was it. Chris had expected open doors and curious citizens, but everyone had remained inside.

"Did we have an aural hallucination?" Ivan asked. "Were we the only ones to hear anything?" He was shoving his feet into a pair of sandals.

Chris shrugged. "Maybe everyone takes their hearing aids out at night?"

"Come on."

Ivan was already jogging across the front yard toward the Taurus while Chris scrounged up both of his flip-flops, fervently wishing there was less jogging and more coffee.

As he pulled Frank's front door shut behind himself, Chris asked, "Where are we going anyway?" It was o'dark thirty in the middle of the night, not a time he was intimately familiar with these days.

"Trying to find out what happened," Ivan said. "Obviously."

"Obviously," repeated Chris.

SEVEN

Ivan

Knowing Chris was right behind him, Ivan wrenched open the driver's side door and jammed himself behind the wheel, turning the ignition as he did so. Blue started right up—as always—quiet as a cat. Before Chris could clip his seat belt, Ivan was pulling away from the curb.

"Jesus Christ, Ivan, I'd like to live through the night."

Like always, Ivan planned to drive recklessly, take corners too fast. "Let's do some crimes, Let's get sushi and not pay, thank you very much, Repo Man," he muttered. He'd do about anything to hear Chris growl his name.

"What? Are you still drunk, Morrison?" Chris demanded.

Ivan smirked and pressed his foot against the gas pedal. He wanted to hear his name from Chris's lips all the time. Every day. Forever. Out of the corner of his eye, he saw Chris grab for the panic strap. Fine.

"Braking now." Ivan risked another glance at Chris. "Don't worry, I have plans and they don't include the emergency room. But first, let's figure out where those hogs went."

His plans for Chris were more *hopes* than anything else, but the hope was stronger than it had been when he'd arrived.

"And just how are we going to do that? They're nowhere in sight."

"Let's drive around a bit, maybe we'll run across some unlawful behavior. With luck, they will be in the middle of it. Who shoots off weapons in the middle of a mobile home park?"

"Probably lots of people. Do not run over anyone here—that is a direct order."

"As if," Ivan scoffed, his attention back on the street in front of him. "When have I ever?"

"I'm serious, Ivan. We're not on the job, and killing senior citizens is frowned upon."

"Most of them are asleep in front of their TVs. We'll just drive through the hood for a look-see."

He was going for reassuring but damn, it didn't seem to be working. Chris Hatch was wound a tad tight some days. Most days. He needed to loosen up a bit, and Ivan was the man for the job.

"We are not here in an official capacity, please remember that. We are regular citizens."

"Yes, boss," Ivan snarked.

"You know," Chris said thoughtfully, seeming to ignore the boss comment, "when you called the other day, I was mildly entertained by a senior motorcycle gang that stopped at the house sort of kitty-corner from Frank's place. The shots were close by, let's head that way."

Morrison slowed Blue to a snail's pace and, with great care, executed a three point-turn, then headed back toward Frank's address.

"Which house was it?" he asked.

Hatch pointed to an older version of a single-wide similar to Susie and Lance's, its front door angled away from where Chris was staying. Morrison swung a left and pulled to a stop in front of the home. There were fewer lights on inside the surrounding homes now, and the hum of HVAC units filled the air like a swarm of cicadas.

"Maybe they do all take their hearing aids out, then turn up the AC?" Morrison said, peering into the dark. "I bet no one hears much. Does it look to you like the door is open?"

The longer he stared at the front door, the more it looked to him like it might be ajar, just a crack. Could have also been his imagination.

"Possibly," Chris allowed after peering at the modular home's front door for several seconds.

"We should check. You know, just in case. It's the right thing to do." Ivan wanted to go busting in there, but he would play it cool for Hatch.

"Alright." Chris drew the word out slowly. "But I'll take the lead. It's late, and whoever lives here may have just forgotten to shut the door properly."

"In that case, we need to be neighborly and alert them. Who knows the types of folks around here?" Except for Susie and Lance, who were obviously cool and on the up and up.

Chris narrowed his eyes at him. "I'm going first."

"Sure, sure," Ivan agreed easily.

There was no way Ivan was letting Hatch go in first; he'd been a desk man for too long. But Ivan would let him insist he wanted to go first all he wanted.

Together they got out of Big Blue. When they reached the door and Chris tried to take the lead, Ivan stepped in front of him.

"Take the left side," Ivan ordered.

Amazingly, Chris moved to the left. Ivan took what he considered the more dangerous right side.

"Ready?" he asked, his back pressed against the siding and his right arm outstretched.

Chris nodded.

Raising his fist, Ivan rapped his knuckles against the slightly open door. No response. The house was silent in a way that felt empty. No soft, snuffling sounds of a person asleep, just a sort of abandonment.

"Do you hear anything?" Chris asked quietly.

"I don't think so." Ivan banged harder on the door. It moved infinitesimally. If there was someone inside, they weren't answering.

"The lock isn't engaged," Chris pointed out, as if Ivan hadn't figured that out for himself.

Not wanting to get gut-shot, Ivan kicked the door with the back of his heel, forcing it further open.

"There's something blocking it," Chris muttered.

"Hello? Anyone there?" Ivan called out quietly.

He cocked his head, listening, but there was definitely no answer. The house felt deserted, unoccupied, as if no one had been inside for days, if not weeks. But was it empty? If so, why had the door been ajar? And why had some bikers been poking around? That couldn't be good. Wary, Ivan peeked around the door frame and blinked several times at what he saw in the dim light from the single streetlight nearby.

A human-shaped foot connected to an oddly orange leg kept the door from opening all the way. Ivan stared at it, trying the make sense of the foot and leg from the angle he was at, but it proved impossible.

"Police, we're coming in," Ivan called out in a more normal tone.

He didn't have his normal door-busting gear, so he pulled his phone out and turned on the flashlight function.

"Police?" Chris whispered. Ivan knew he was gawking at him. "Jesus Christ, Ivan."

"You said not to say we're not here in an official capacity," Ivan hissed back.

"I meant... oh for fuck's sake, open the door."

Ivan used his larger mass to push the door open against the weight of the leg. Because in the end that's all it was—a leg. A leg that looked like one of those attached to clothing store mannequins if the angle at the top of it was anything to go by. He tipped his phone downward to get a better look. Except this appendage appeared to be made out of plaster, not hard plastic, which explained why it was so heavy.

"What the fresh hell is this?" he said.

"Jesus Christ," Chris repeated, also staring down at the lone body part.

"You must be getting old, you sound like a broken record."

"Ha fucking ha."

The front room was shrouded in darkness, one of the few houses that hadn't had a glowing TV illuminating the lonely evening streets. Instead, the heavy curtains were still pulled closed against the blazing sun and the heat it promised come morning. To Ivan's sensitive nose, the house smelled musty, as if it wasn't currently lived in—or the occupant wasn't a great housekeeper. He blinked, fighting off a sneeze.

Bringing his phone up again, Ivan bit back the scream building at the back of his throat.

Eyes, many of them, stared back at them. So. Many. Eyes.

Breathing in through his nose, Ivan worked to calm his pounding heart. Whatever the eyes were, they weren't alive, at least not anymore. And Ivan was pretty sure they weren't human.

"What the actual fuck." Chris really needed to be more imaginative with his cursing.

"Taxidermy," said Ivan. "One of my creepier uncles was into it. He even did snakes, which are really fucking difficult. The really good taxidermists paint each scale by hand to make them look more realistic. Less dead."

Slowly, Ivan panned the room with his phone, the light from the flash app reaching through the murky dark to illuminate a menagerie of beasts. The light didn't go far, so the creatures—it seemed to Ivan anyway—resolved into whatever the fuck they were and then disappeared again as he moved his phone along.

The remains, for lack of a better descriptor, hung from the walls, stood on their own feet (or in some cases, lay on their sides or backs), and loomed from every corner. At first glance, he spotted several owls, possibly a fox, a couple of coyotes. A six-foot alligator—maybe a crocodile, he never had gotten them straight—was propped up lengthwise against some shelves. In a distant corner, a badger, or who knew, maybe it was a fucking wolverine, bared its sharp teeth at them.

In the jumble, it was difficult to tell whether the stuffed creatures had been arranged that way or if someone or someones had rifled through them. The odd musty odor in the air that Ivan assumed had to do with the carcasses was really starting to bother him.

"Is this legal?" Chris asked. "Never mind, I don't want to know."

Ivan doubted that what they were looking at was entirely legal. His uncle used to "procure" endangered species for clients and, like the weirdos who had to have their own DaVinci or van Gogh, his customers often wanted their own condor, bald eagle, or Bengal tiger.

"People are weird," was all he could come up with.

Bending down, Chris tugged the plaster leg out of the way of the door, grunting at its weight, and stepped inside.

"Seriously, what the fuck is all this?" he asked, using his own phone light to look around.

Surely that was a rhetorical question.

"Ya got me, boss."

"Stop it with the boss stuff," Chris grumbled. "I think we're past that."

"What if I like calling you boss?" Ivan teased, bumping Chris with his shoulder.

Chris pinched the bridge of his nose. "My god, what have I gotten myself into with you? Obviously, that was a rhetorical question."

"So much good stuff." Ivan shot him a lascivious grin. "I've just been hanging around waiting for you to see me."

"That's what scares me. Regardless of your intent, which I approve of, what the hell is going on here?" Chris asked. "We should probably have a look and make sure there's no human body hanging around."

"Alright, if you insist. But you and I both know if there is a body around here, it's been decades since it was alive. And this person doesn't do his work here, or he buys it at estate sales and shit like that."

"Huh. Well, since the door was open, let's do a check just to make sure no one's here."

Chris pushed past the leg and into the house. Rolling his eyes at Chris's back, Ivan followed him. The man just had to prove he was in charge, didn't he? Admittedly, Ivan liked that about Chris Hatch.

There were no live bodies and no dead humans. There was no one else in the home, just Ivan, Chris, and a couple hundred creepy preserved creatures. The kitchen was clean, the fridge empty. A stack of flyers and envelopes on a scarred side table told them that someone named Cleevus Buckley had at least had his mail sent there at some point.

"Postmark on this one is mid-January," Chris said after looking at the envelope on the top of the small pile.

"Maybe he has his mail held until he picks it up. I bet the association here offers that service."

"Okay, but then why were the bikers here the other day? They knocked as if they expected someone to answer the door for them."

"That I cannot say."

Aside from the fucking plaster leg by the door and the creepy animals with their beady plastic eyes, there were odd pieces of terracotta pottery stashed around the home too. Morrison assumed they were supposed to be art, but who really knew?

Suns and moons, candle holders, a chess set. Planters, pots, weird sculptures. He was reminded of the masturbating frog he'd seen. Perhaps this was the artist? The pieces were every-where, propped up against the walls in the bedroom, in the kitchen, in the closets. There was even a box of them in the bathroom. In addition to the first leg, there were several more appendages—hands, feet, full arms, and even more legs—scat-tered across the carpeted floor.

"I don't see how a person could live here. There's hardly enough room to move around." Ivan felt like he was about to knock something over and send everything to the floor in domino fashion, adding to what was already there.

"This place is extra creepy, right?" Ivan asked Chris. "It is, isn't it? It's not just me? Is Cleevus auditioning for the part of serial killer in the newest Netflix series?"

"There's nothing here except—well, no dead or injured humans anyway," Chris agreed. "And since you asked, it *is* fucking creepy. Whoever this Buckley guy is, he likes to collect extremely bizarre stuff."

"What if there are real people parts inside those plaster molds? Ugh, I'm ready to get out of here."

Turning, Chris slow-blinked at him before responding. "Real people parts? Isn't the taxidermy shit bad enough? Seriously, Ivan." He took one last look around before pulling the front door shut behind them. "I still think the gunshots came from here though. And I'd like to know why."

Back behind the steering wheel of Big Blue, Ivan drove through the neighborhood again and then covered a six-block radius outside it, but the hogs were gone and there was no immediate evidence of uproar. Not that they found anyway.

"Fine, let's get back to Frank's place," Chris finally said. "I'm tired and my mom will be knocking on the door before eight a.m. I can't believe you agreed to breakfast."

"And the Grand Canyon," Ivan reminded Chris.

"*Maybe* the Grand Canyon."

"Right, first figure out what's going on with Cleevus, then the Grand Canyon."

Chris groaned, but Ivan knew he was right.

EIGHT

Chris

Chris's eyes popped open. Slowly, the speckled popcorn ceiling of Frank-the-Neighbor's bedroom came into focus, and for a millisecond, he wondered if the night before had been a wild dream. First, the surprise that was Ivan Morrison, and then later, a house of horrors.

No, the contents of the house had not been a dream. He could still smell them. The odd scent lingered uninvited, making him want to take another shower.

And then there was Ivan.

Maybe his mom had slipped some love potion into their drinks. But no, even if Chris believed a potion might work—which he did not—his parents would never do something like that.

Therefore, last night had really happened. He and Ivan Morrison had made out and slept in the same bed. The soft shuffle and shift of the warm body turning over and pressing up next to him in the bed reinforced his conclusion. He and Ivan had "slept together." Been intimate.

It had been a lack of supplies that slowed them down—which Chris was thankful for this morning. He wasn't afraid to admit he wanted Ivan in the most carnal of ways, but he wanted to be sober.

Swiping his hand down his face, Chris blinked himself awake. The familiar morning stubble on his cheeks scraped against his palm and helped him to think, to focus.

Ivan Morrison had happened.

He ran through a mental checklist: Panic, no. Regret, no. Slept? Yes.

Maybe it hadn't been a terrible idea to give in to their mutual attraction, but they were going to have to sort out the boss-employee issue.

Almost-sex had been followed by the sound of gunshots, the discovery of an open front door, and a freakish collection of *something*. But they'd found no body and no evidence of foul play. After they'd not exactly broken into the neighbor's, Ivan had insisted on cruising around again once they'd left the house. They hadn't found anything. Not a motor-trike in sight.

Another thought struck him. Would Ivan worry that it had been the drinks that Susie had handed out like Halloween candy which had led to Chris giving in to their chemistry? Hopefully not. The reality was, they'd been orbiting each other for a while now. Ever since Morrison had, quite literally, exploded into Chris's universe. And, recognizing temptation for what it was, Chris had immediately slammed all his mental and emotional doors against Ivan.

Besides, they'd worked together.

Chris would be the first to admit he'd done everything possible to *not* see Ivan, even going so far as to convince himself he was in love with Dante Castone. Chris did believe he and Dante could've been good together—if they both weren't so damned stubborn, and if Andre hadn't gotten there first.

It had been too easy for Chris to imagine that he and the ex-undercover agent had a connection that was more than friendship. Which in turn had made it easy to avoid any real relationships because Dante was rarely around and Chris was his boss. It made everything so much easier.

Ivan was not easy. He was not simple and malleable. Dante wasn't either, but Chris had to be honest with himself finally; he hadn't been in love with Dante at all, he'd just been avoiding... Ivan.

Chris had known he was in trouble last winter when he'd come down with a nasty bout of the flu. Ivan had shown up at his house with a gallon of Tom Yum soup and steamed dumplings, then proceeded to make him drink fluids and eat until he could function again. The house had felt empty after he'd left.

"Did last night really happen?" Ivan's deep voice was raspy from sleep. "We broke the seal and then stumbled upon the downright weirdest fucking art I have ever seen in my life?"

"Broke the seal?" Chris, of course, immediately focused on Ivan's choice of words.

Ivan rolled over onto his side, his lips curved into a smug grin.

"You know exactly what I mean... boss."

"Oh my god. No. I can't be your boss anymore."

"Meh, don't get all worked up. I told you I'm transferring to what's his name—Madison's—team."

"You mean Radisson? Also, no, you didn't say anything, I would not have forgotten."

"Oh. Huh. Sorry about that. The transfer is fairly simple since we're in the same jurisdiction, and it's not like I haven't worked on feeb teams in the past. But, yeah, Andrew Radisson, FBI guy, that's right. Good guy. It's all good. Everything is very good. Should be done by the time we get back."

Clearly, Ivan was not at all worried that either of them might have been influenced by an outside force known as vodka lemonade.

"Frankly, Andy has no idea what he's getting into with you," Chris said thoughtfully, amused by Ivan's deflection—he knew Radisson's name as well as he knew his own.

"He's not getting into anything with me. That's your job now." It was possible that Ivan's grin grew even wider.

"Is that so? Is that why we're 'getting a place together' when we get back? I still can't believe you said that to my parents."

"Your place is alright. But I think between the two of us, we could find something better. When you're ready."

Chris rolled his eyes and laughed. "I'm just supposed to go from being a hard-hearted bachelor to—"

"To mine." Ivan pointed a thick finger at his own chest. The chest Chris very much enjoyed while running his fingers through Ivan's silky chest hair. "Zero to sixty, baby."

He let that roll around in his head for a minute. Was he panicked? No. *Huh.* After all, his parents had, as they'd told Ivan, met at a Grateful Dead show and rarely been apart since. Maybe it was his DNA.

"Ugh, my parents." Chris sighed, sinking further back onto his pillow. One voice in his head whispered, *This is too soon, it's not real*, while another, louder voice reminded him that he and Ivan had known each other for literal years, so it was not too soon at all.

Calm the fuck down, son.

"What about your folks?" Ivan asked.

"My parents will be happy." Chris knew he sounded like this was tragic news. They already were happy about Ivan.

"Wouldn't want that now, would we? Your parents being happy for you. What a fucking tragedy," Ivan teased.

Chris knew from past conversations that Ivan's parents

hadn't spoken to him since he came out. They would never be happy for him. They had no idea how incredible their son was. Chris hated them.

"Fuck off," he retorted mildly. "You know it's not that."

"Joy is not a bad thing," Ivan pointed out. "Are you allergic to being happy? Before you answer, remember I saw every single picture of you that your mom has in her possession last night."

"No, I'm not allergic to being happy." He stared up at the ceiling again. "I guess it was hard growing up with them... being happy all the time. Knowing that no way was I ever going to be as happy as they were."

"Ah, so you're a glass-is-half-empty-and-about-to-be-knocked-over guy? I already knew that about you. And also—" Ivan lifted himself up onto his forearms, leaned over, and claimed Chris's mouth for his own for a moment before saying, "I make you happy."

Chris had a response for that, but Ivan quickly covered his mouth with his large hand, making it impossible to speak.

"Mmph."

"Don't say whatever you want to say. We'll just get ourselves up, head over to your folks for the breakfast we were promised, then see where the day takes us. Okay? We don't need to set a damn wedding date or whatever else is on your mind. We'll just be Chris and Ivan. Hatch and Morrison."

Chris nodded and Ivan took his hand away.

"Oxygen deprivation is not really the way to woo someone."

"Oh," Ivan said. "Really? Hmm." He swung his legs off the bed. "Coffee? You do have that here, don't you? Even I don't think I can face Susie and Lance without a cup of the holy brew."

He was only wearing boxers, and since he was mostly naked, Chris took the time to appreciate the wonder that was

Ivan. Solid. Unmovable. And yet he could move damn quickly when he needed to apprehend a perp or keep a random toddler from dashing off the sidewalk. His broad and hair-covered chest had a few scars here and there, and a tattoo of—

"Is that from *The Lion King?*" This was the first time he'd gotten a good look at the normally covered-up ink.

Ivan looked down at his pec. "It's the warthog. I have an affinity for warthogs. They just don't get enough appreciation. They're fierce, cute, a little chubby, and have those little tails. But seriously, is there coffee?" he asked while rummaging in his duffle bag to find a clean t-shirt and a pair of cargo shorts.

"Yes," Chris said after watching him for a minute, "there's a bag of pre-ground in the freezer. Hang on."

Ivan's shorts were on already and the shirt was halfway over his head. He pulled the shirt all the way down and his head popped through the neck opening like a goofy jack-in-the-box.

"Take your time, I'll get the coffee going." Ivan shot him a brilliant smile that left Chris a bit breathless.

He didn't want to take his time. He had an unreasonable fear that if he left Ivan on his own, he would disappear. Or prove to have been a figment of Chris's imagination. Or worse, that Chris would somehow ruin everything, whatever this everything was. Taking a deep breath, he tamped down his anxiety with breathing exercises. When he felt slightly better, Chris rolled out of bed, got out a clean pair of shorts and an old DEA training t-shirt, and made his way into the kitchen.

"GOOD MORNING, YOU TWO!" Susie sang out.

Chris never could fully comprehend how his mom seemed to defy all medical science by never appearing to be hungover. His dad was definitely moving a little slower this morning but perked up when he saw Chris and Ivan.

"Morning, son. Ivan. Have a seat. Actually," Lance said, swiveling toward the side door, "let's sit out back. This kitchen is too small for all four of us, and the dining room table is reserved for the puzzle of the month." Rising to his feet, Lance led the way to the kitchen door and the patio.

"Lance, take the orange juice out with you. I'll bring the coffee, I think I have a carafe around here somewhere."

"Let me help carry something, Susie." Ivan offered.

"Aren't you a darling." His mom opened one of the upper cupboards and pointed to the top shelf, where a large silver thermos sat. "Grab that and we'll fill it up. Coffee cups are over there. I've got a frittata in the oven that will be done in just a few minutes."

Following his dad out to the patio, Chris couldn't help but smile. His mom had been watching Frank-the-Neighbor's door and put the frittata in to cook as soon as she saw them step outside.

"Have a seat," Lance said, setting the glass pitcher down on the patio table. "OJ?"

"Sure."

Orange juice had always been part of his parents' breakfast routine; every morning growing up, Chris had started the day with a glass of orange juice. Probably, Susie had thought it might improve his mood. It had not.

The back door opened again, and Ivan emerged, carrying the large flask in one hand and four mugs in the other. "Coffee, anyone?" he called out in a jovial tone.

Chris felt himself smile. Coffee, on the other hand, cheered him right up—or maybe it was the Ivan Morrison Effect.

Affect? Whatever.

Setting the thermos and mugs down, Ivan proceeded to fill them one by one. "You should take the first one," he said to

Chris. "I know it always takes you two or three cups to start your morning where a normal person does."

"Ha fucking ha," said Chris as he proceeded to snatch the first cup out of his dad's reach.

"Mr. Hatch, I apologize for your son's manners."

Sitting back in his chair, Lance chuckled. "Chris has great manners. But you're right about the coffee."

Ivan moved one of the chairs closer to Chris's and sat down next to him, stretching his legs out as far as he could underneath the table.

"Are you comfortable yet?" Chris asked.

Ivan smiled and bumped his shoulder against Chris's. "Yes."

"Did you two sleep all right over there?" Lance asked.

Before Chris could think of anything to say, Ivan's large palm landed on his thigh and squeezed.

"Yep. It's not the bed I'm used to at home, but it will do for a few days."

"What do you two have planned for the day? Anything?"

"I want to see the Grand Canyon while I'm here—could we do that tomorrow? Chris and I have some business to look into this morning."

"Great idea! We have a pass," Lance said, "and of course we don't go as often as we should."

"Do you know the person who lives at the place around the corner from you?"

"The one sort of across from Frank's?" Lance asked.

"Yes, the place with the fat Buddha statue in the front yard," Ivan elaborated.

"Oh." Lance's eyebrows drew together. "*That place.* Supposedly, the owner travels a lot, so I've never officially met him, only seen him from afar a few times. Susie might have. He has an odd name, I remember that."

The back door opened again, and Ivan hopped up to take the casserole from Susie.

"I'll be right back with the plates. Don't talk about anything else without me!"

Exchanging smiles, they all obeyed the directive, sitting quietly in the Arizona sunshine for a minute and sipping at their coffee. The next time Susie came bustling outside, she carried a stack of plastic plates, forks, and napkins.

"Okay," she said, setting down everything and plopping down next to her husband. "Continue. What were you talking about?"

"Ivan wants to visit the canyon, but he also asked about Frank's neighbor. Clive?"

"Cleevus, Cleevus Buckley. Here you go, Ivan." She handed him a spatula. "Help yourself and pass it along."

Chris watched Ivan take a tiny serving and set it on his plate before holding the dish out to him.

"Take more than that," he said quietly. "Mom is going to be pissed if you pass out from hunger. No reason to be shy here, it's not like I don't know what it takes to keep that engine going."

Ivan glared at him. "I'll have you know, I am being polite. You have heard of this practice?"

"Fine, have it your way." Chris took a huge spoonful and put it on his own plate. If there was any left, Ivan could have it. Maybe he'd been taught to take a small first serving so everyone got some, but from what little Chris knew about his family, he doubted that was the case.

It seemed more likely that it had been every person for themselves at the Morrison kitchen table. It had never occurred to Chris that Morrison might have food issues. He wondered if he'd been food-shamed as a child. Another wash of anger at the way Morrison had been treated growing up rushed through him, and Chris had to take a gulp of hot coffee to wash it back down.

"You okay?" Ivan asked.

"Hunky dory. Let's talk about the neighbor some more. I'm sure that doesn't happen much around here. You all mind your own business and pay no attention to what's going on. Am I right, Mom?"

"Christopher," Susie said, her eyebrows drawing together, "of course we don't mind our own business. What do you want to know about Cleevus?"

Between the two of them, Ivan and Chris shared what had happened the night before. Not *everything*—Chris would have rather stuck needles in his eye than talk personal details with his parents. But they told them about the noise and finding the door unlocked.

"It was ajar," explained Ivan, "or we never would've gone inside. Like a wellness check kind of thing."

"Right," Chris said, even though they had no authority in Arizona. "A wellness check."

"Good," said Susie. "Finding someone dead would be horrible. Although those creatures must have given you a scare."

Ivan and Chris exchanged a glance and eyebrow raises—as if between Chris and Ivan, they hadn't seen many dead bodies and caused some of them too.

"No dead bodies," Ivan continued. "But aside from the taxidermy, there was a lot of terracotta stuff. Also a plaster leg."

"Oh, well, those aren't weird. Frank's neighbor sells the pots and 'art' at some of the local markets," Susie said. "I think he goes around and buys things from garage sales and estates, calls himself a picker. Like on that show, *American Pickers*. Most of it's crap."

"He's not selling any inventory he left behind. Have you seen him in a while?" Chris asked his mom.

Thinking for a minute, Susie washed down her bite of frittata with a swig of orange juice.

"We haven't seen him recently, have we, Lance? But so many people here are snowbirds, they're in and out all the time."

Lance was nodding. "I don't think we have seen him. Honestly, I don't know if I could tell you what he looks like other than he's white, average height, probably in his late sixties or early seventies, but with being in the sun a lot, he could be younger. Not under fifty, of course. Dark-haired once, but now more salt than pepper."

Trust his dad "not to know what someone looked like" and still provide an excellent description of them.

"Is he friendly with anyone here?" Ivan asked.

His parents both shook their heads and shrugged. "I can't say," Susie replied. "But you could ask at the clubhouse."

"We could also ask around at the market in the town center. I think he has a booth there," offered Lance.

Oh, great. Lance Hatch, retired city librarian, was on the case. And worse, his dad's keen instincts were sending Chris and Ivan to a shopping area infested with people.

"Thanks for the tip, Dad," Chris said, meaning it, "but just Ivan and I will head over there to ask questions."

NINE

Ivan

"Cleevus Buckley. Now there's a name I haven't heard in a hot minute."

The wizened older person selling kettle corn appeared thoughtful. The kettle corn booth was directly next to the space Cleevus Buckley apparently usually rented.

"I haven't seen him around for a while now." He closed one eye as he tried to remember. "Maybe a couple weeks? Maybe longer? But he could be shacked up with that woman he's been seeing, she seems like she has money. Cleevus likes the money."

Ivan almost laughed out loud when the man said *shacked up*. Who used terms like that these days? This guy, apparently. The light breeze changed directions, and Ivan's stomach rumbled in response to the heady scent of gourmet-style popcorn actively assaulting his senses.

Later. After they got the information they needed.

"By any chance does she ride a bike?" Chris asked, oblivious to Ivan's intense desire for a midmorning snack.

"I don't know about that. It's weird that Cleevus hasn't been around now that you mention it. He doesn't like to miss snow-bird season."

"Oh, yeah?" Chris said. "Any particular reason why?"

"His freaky stuff is popular with the tourists. My corn sells all year round," he said proudly.

There was something about the way he said "stuff" that had Ivan thinking about taxidermy and yard art.

"His taxidermy or the terracotta pieces? The frogs?" asked Ivan, picturing the frog he'd seen near Chris's borrowed address.

"Those frogs, man. They're twisted, but I swear the ladies snap 'em up. They sell like hot cakes when he has new ones. People think they're the funniest things they've ever seen."

"He doesn't sell the stuffed animals? The taxidermy?" Chris clarified.

The popcorn guy didn't answer immediately. He squeezed one eye shut, his gaze shifting back and forth while he considered the question.

"Not as far as I know. Leastways, not here at the market."

Ivan was tempted to push for more but something made him hesitate. Instead, he asked again, "And he hasn't been around lately?"

"Nope." The man shook his head. "Like I said, not for a while."

"Thanks for the information," Chris said, getting ready to turn away.

"We'll take a small bag of corn," said Ivan. "Nah, make it a medium."

The vendor's grin was missing several teeth but it was bright. Quickly and efficiently, he filled a bag and handed it over. Ivan slipped him a twenty.

"We appreciate you talking to us. Don't worry about the change."

Opening the bag, Ivan held it out toward Chris as they continued making their way down the aisle of booths.

After hesitating for a second, Chris dug in and took a handful, popping it into his mouth.

The popcorn vendor had been the third person they'd talked to, and the consensus was that Cleevus Buckley being MIA at this time of year was not normal. If it had been summer, people might not have noticed, but this was just the beginning of high tourist season. Spring training was coming up and Buckley was not out hawking his wares.

"Wow," said Chris around his crunchy treat. "This stuff is amazing."

"You've never had kettle corn before?" Ivan asked.

"Nope."

"Well, keeping hanging around with me, and I'll make sure you try all sorts of new things."

Chris shot him a grin. "Promises, promises."

Ivan mentally replayed what he'd just said. "I didn't mean—ugh." Giving up, he shoved a big handful of the popcorn into his mouth so he wouldn't say anything else stupid. However, if saying shit like that meant he got a grin out of Chris Hatch? Then he'd never stop.

"What made you ask about frogs?" Chris asked when he'd swallowed.

"Oh, yeah. When I got here yesterday, I noticed your buddy Frank has a masturbating frog in his front yard."

"A masturbating frog? Seriously?" Chris's voice rose. "And he's not my buddy, I've never met the man."

"Want to go check it out? I think we're done here, don't you?" Ivan knew Chris would be horrified by the self-pleasuring amphibian. Hatch wasn't so much a prude as hyper focused on his work, causing him to miss the fringes—the lacey bits.

"Yeah, let's get out of here. It's starting to get hot. I have to say, this vacation I'm on is becoming more fun by the minute. Motorcycle gangs, taxidermy, masturbating frogs. What's next?"

IVAN PARKED Blue where he had when he'd arrived the day before, in the shadow of a large palm tree.

"It's right there." Ivan pointed at the terracotta amphibian clearly jacking off.

Chris peered out the car window. "Huh. You weren't kidding." He sounded amazed, as if he might have thought Ivan had been exaggerating.

"I never said I was kidding."

"Yeah, I know that, but I'd kind of hoped you were."

"Nope." He turned off Blue's engine and turned to look at Chris.

Chris was staring across the street at the possibly missing taxidermist's house.

"I wonder..." His voice trailed off.

Ivan loved watching Chris Hatch think. It was almost better than sex, the way he nibbled at his lower lip, his jaw flexed. It was almost more than Ivan could take.

"What do you know about taxidermy? Did your creepy uncle ever tell you anything?"

"Uncle Scott? He could be dead by now. One can always hope anyway. I don't know much about the process really. I do know there are some animals people need permits to stuff, and some need to be tested for diseases they are known to carry so humans don't get sick. And endangered species are a big no-no. Which is why they always claim, 'Oh no, Mister Fish and Wildlife Officer, I just found this perfectly intact northern spotted owl lying in the road.'"

"Maybe our friend Cleevus got mixed up with the wrong kind of people?"

"The kind who deal in black market shit?" Ivan asked.

"Or he could be the wrong kind of people. Is that a thing in taxidermy?"

"Sure." Ivan nodded. "Just like in the art world, there are freakos out there who want to own the last white rhino and will pay big money to acquire it just so they can stuff the thing and display it in their massive jack-off library. Also exotics and endangered things like sperm whale penises."

"Sperm whale penises?" Again Chris sounded shocked.

"There's a penis museum in Iceland," Ivan explained. "They don't have human ones, I don't think. We should go."

Chris didn't immediately respond, processing, Ivan assumed, things like taxidermized penises and going to a museum in Iceland together. "Well, while that is interesting," he finally said, "and maybe information I never needed to know, look around you. This retirement community doesn't scream big money to me. Does it to you? Are residents here clamoring for grizzly bear dicks or out hunting the last known Tasmanian tiger? No."

Ivan was impressed that Chris brought up the long-extinct creature. He did have a point about the community though. These were people living on a fixed income, not highflyers.

"Might be a good cover for him," Ivan said. "Who would suspect some rando living in a fifty-and-up community to be dealing in black-market stuffed creatures? But maybe it's not the animals. It could be the terracotta," he added. "If I was smuggling something, it seems like in those would be a way to do it without getting noticed. That stuff is everywhere."

"You could be onto something there. What if our friend Cleevus was the middle man for something small enough to hide in pottery—"

"Or a taxidermized owl," Ivan interjected.

"Or a taxidermized bird." Chris actually rolled his eyes. "And instead of passing it along, he took it for himself."

"Okay, but then what? Someone found out and—and what? Offed the guy? Why would a bunch of MCs drop by to say hi if he's dead? Maybe he's enjoying a vacation somewhere far away?"

"They don't know he's gone. He's probably not dead. He could have scarpered."

"Scarpered?" Ivan frowned and stared over at Chris. "What kind of word is that?"

"A good one when we're discussing taxidermy and seventy-year-olds."

"Why didn't they trash the place, then?" Ivan asked. "Why shoot off their weapons?"

"No idea there."

"If they didn't want to alert Cleevus that they're onto him, the guns were a bad idea. If he knows someone is looking for him, he might decide to permanently disappear."

Even in the shade, Big Blue was heating up fast in the Arizona heat. Ivan shifted to open the door, automatically glancing in the rearview mirror first.

"Or," he said, "we could talk to them. This is them, am I right?" A group of five motorcycles rumbled up behind them and came to a stop in front of Cleevus's house. "How about first we sit tight and see what they're up to? If they're up to no good, they aren't being very sneaky about it," Ivan pointed out.

"Does it look to you like anyone around here cares? They could come in blazing like Clint Eastwood, and if hearing aids were turned off, no one would hear them. Plus, it's community time," Chris said. "My folks are probably playing Ping-Pong or something, and I bet they aren't the only ones."

Ivan watched the group of motorcycle riders slowly dismount.

They weren't all senior citizens, but something about the front man pinged his radar. He wasn't sure what it was about him—the shape of his shoulders, maybe. His movements, even as an obviously older man, were much like a tiger's. Not a lion. Lions were inherently lazy and believed they deserved to rule their kingdom. Lions expected to be fawned over, adored. Tigers though. Tigers inherently knew they were the apex predator and they would fight to prove it, but they rarely had to. They didn't care about being adored or fawned over, they were the supreme ruler.

"Did you tell me what their colors were?" he asked.

"No, that's not my area of expertise."

All the "real" MCs had colors. For instance, Hell's Angels colors were red letters on a white background with a skull of some kind, leading to them also being known as the red and white.

Ivan had spent a few years early in his undercover career trying to get close to Gunnar Sinclair, close enough to catch a motorcycle club president doing something they could get him behind bars for. He'd never been caught with the proverbial smoking gun, and Ivan had been called back, the operation dropped.

And then, a few years ago, the guy had dropped off the radar completely. The Velvet Devils MC was still around, but Gunnar Sinclair was not at the helm and they no longer dabbled in sex and drug trafficking. Instead, the MC raised money for children's hospitals, animal rescues and, randomly, STEM scholarship programs.

"That's Gunnar Sinclair," Ivan said. "I'd bet my retirement fund on it. He was on our watch list for years. Murder, drugs, sex trafficking—those are just some of the things he was suspected of, if not actively doing, at least ordering to be done."

"What the hell is he doing here?" Chris asked. "In broad daylight?"

"Probably what most everybody else is, trying to enjoy his sunset years. That's a nice bike he's got there," Ivan noted. "We were never able to pin anything on him, although we have a few lower-level Velvet Devils behind bars, plus his son."

"You're sure it's him?" Chris asked. "One hundred percent positive?"

Keeping his attention on the rearview mirror, Ivan didn't bother to reply, just raised one eyebrow and reached for the door handle.

"How about I ask him?"

"Don't you fucking dare."

Ivan didn't open the door, but also didn't remove his hand. "Here in the middle of a retirement community, I don't think he means any harm. Does he look like he means harm to you? Do any of them?"

Chris sucked in a bunch of oxygen as if there was a fire sale on the stuff and then released it.

"No, it doesn't look that way."

"Look," Ivan said. "It's getting hot in Big Blue, so we can't stay inside here anyway. Who knows how long they're going to hang around? Let's just calmly get out and say hello to them like normal people."

"For one thing," Chris said sourly, "I do not randomly say hello to people."

"Of course you don't, Agent Hatch, but how about just this once." Ivan pushed the door open and got out of the car.

The thud of Blue's doors shutting had the riders turning to look at Ivan and Chris.

"Howdy," Ivan called out as he crossed the street to get closer to them. Behind him, he could hear Chris muttering threats under his breath. "Not my boss," he said out the side of his mouth.

"I'll be having a conversation with your boss," Chris promised.

"Morning," a rider, younger than the rest, said. "Well, afternoon by now, I guess."

"Are you looking for"—Ivan turned to Chris—"what's his name again?" He had kept moving and was now about twenty feet from Gunnar Sinclair himself. Even in his sixties, the man had power, a draw Ivan could feel.

"Cleevus. Cleevus Buckley," Chris responded to Ivan.

The younger guy abandoned Gunnar, moving to meet Ivan and Chris. "Have you seen him recently?" the stranger asked. "We've been by a couple of times with no luck."

"Chris," Ivan said over his shoulder, not wanting to turn his back on them just yet, "you've been here a bit longer than me. Have you seen Cleevus?"

Chris reached Ivan's side, standing so they were now shoulder to shoulder.

"Nope. I saw you guys a few days ago though."

Ivan silently wished Chris didn't sound exactly like the DEA agent he was.

"Oh yeah, we stopped by." He stuck out his hand. "Tyrone Duke, it's nice to meet you."

Tyrone was possibly in his late thirties or early forties but had one of those faces that made it hard to tell.

"It's a pleasure, Tyrone. Ivan Morrison, and this guy here is Chris Hatch."

Gunnar separated from the rest of the group to join the three of them at the end of Buckley's driveway. He slung an arm around the younger man and pulled him close. Smiling, Tyrone glanced up at him, affection and possibly love in his gaze. What the hell was going on here? Last Ivan had known, the Velvet Devils were not rainbow friendly.

"Knock it off with the protective stuff, Gunnar." But Tyrone didn't pull away, instead leaning into the older man.

"Do I know you from somewhere?" Gunnar asked, staring intently at Ivan. "I have a damn good memory for names and faces, but I just can't place you."

Ivan opened his mouth to say something, but Tyrone got there first.

"Morrison was sniffing around the club a few years ago, I think. Didn't go by Morrison at the time. Is that a new name or were you undercover?"

Gunnar eyed him warily, but the man wasn't scared. Neither of them were. Ivan watched as recognition flared in his eyes.

"We're here on vacation," Ivan half raised his hands. "Well, to be honest, Chris was here first, and I crashed his PTO. Ivan *is* my real name."

If they were going to pretend to be normal folk just enjoying the Arizona sunshine in late February, then so was he.

"PTO?" asked Gunnar, frowning.

"Personal Time Off," Tyrone explained before Ivan could. "I was corporate for a while before I took over finances for Gunnar's business," he added.

The man under discussion still had one arm around Tyrone, and Ivan noted a small rainbow flag pin affixed to his leather vest. Well, well, well. He let himself relax a little more.

"So, Ivan, what brought you and the fed here?" Gunnar asked.

Chris shifted beside him. Ivan knew he wanted to protest his fed status, but facts were facts.

"Chris's hippie folks live here. His boss forced him to take his vacation time. I followed him so I could woo him and proclaim my undying love."

"For real?" breathed Tyrone, looking back and forth between them. "That is incredibly romantic."

"Jesus Christ," muttered Chris.

Ivan shrugged, but he also kind of wanted to plant one on Chris's gorgeous mouth that second. He restrained himself. "True though."

"Have you?" Gunnar asked.

"Have I what?" The already very weird discussion was getting weirder.

"Declared your undying love?" offered Tyrone.

Ivan glanced at Chris, who looked like he would rather stick a needle in his eye than continue this line of conversation

"I started to last night, but with Chris, I have to go slow. I don't want to scare him off."

"Ivan." *Gah,* his name that way. "I've known you for years now. I don't think you're going to scare me off."

"Yoo-hoo out there, it's really starting to warm up. We've got iced tea and lemonade. Do you want to invite your friends over? There's plenty of extra. We can all fit under the umbrellas on the patio, and Lance will turn on the outdoor fans."

If Chris's parents had been out at the community center, they were home now.

Chris grimaced. "My mother. She's not going to take no for an answer."

"You should know that Gunnar and the rest of us here"—Tyrone waved at the other three riders—"we're all that's left of the Velvet Devils, and we are extremely respectable these days. We give to charity: Reading Rainbow, The Trevor Project, The Garden of Peace Project, The Boys and Girls Club."

"Tyrone is a financial advisor," Gunnar said. "A very good one," he added, his tone proud.

"We'll be right there, Mom," Chris called out. He turned

back to the rest of them. "So, this is neutral ground? What happens in Surprise stays in Surprise?"

"Except for me," Ivan added. He was not going to be part of a list that did not include him and Chris together.

"Except for you, Ivan."

TEN

Apparently, tea with a former motorcycle gang leader was what was next. Chris needed to learn never to ask that question.

"You have a granddaughter?" Susie beamed across the table at Gunnar. "We need to hear all about her."

Chris was having a hard time wrapping his head around the fact that they were sitting around talking about life with the president of the Velvet Devils—who were vastly reformed. Next he knew, they'd be swapping recipes. His mom was going to have Tyrone's and Gunnar's phone numbers programed into her cell before they returned to wherever they were staying—or lived.

They hadn't actually said what they were doing in Surprise yet, or why they'd been by Buckley's numerous times.

"Her name is Hazel, and she is the reason we stopped by the other day and today. She's a real genius, gives her dads and me a run for our money." Gunnar grinned and pulled his cellphone out of a vest pocket, holding it out so they all could see a selfie-style picture of a young girl suited up in a wet suit and snorkel and giving the camera a thumbs-up.

"She's lovely and adventurous," Susie said.

"Thank you. I like to think she takes after me," Gunnar said, settling back into his seat.

The other riders had opted to meet up with Gunnar and Tyrone later that evening instead of joining them. Which was good because, as much as his mother might have wished it, her patio was just not large enough.

"She's also grounded from the internet until she's eighteen," Tyrone added dryly.

"Oh?" Chris said. "What happened?"

Gunnar rolled his eyes. "Somehow, Hazel found out about this neighbor of yours, Cleevus Buckley, from the internet. Took her about two seconds to figure out he's selling black-market taxidermy, and she packed to come down here on her own and torch the place. I think she gets that from me. Luckily, Dutch and Foster stopped her just as she was boarding the ferry. Dutch called and I promised her we'd talk to him."

"Ah, but even better than you, er, talking to him," Ivan said before Chris did, "we have legal resources. After what we saw last night, Chris is putting a call into Fish and Game."

"I am?" Chris asked.

"You definitely are. We both saw what he has in there. Not. Legal. Some of that I bet people can't even possess."

They'd work out the legality of their accidental search later. They had been doing a legitimate wellness check after all.

"Fine. I guess I'm making a call."

"She sounds wonderful, Gunnar," Susie said. "I can tell you're very proud of her."

"We both are." Gunnar shot Tyrone a glance so full of tenderness that Chris had to blink at its brilliance. "Hazel is all about protecting endangered animals and resources, she's our very own... what's that young woman's name?" he asked Tyrone.

"Greta Thunburg," Tyrone said. "If her dads ever un-ground her, we plan on taking Hazel on a trip to Iceland and Norway, see some puffins and maybe Beluga whales."

"Yeah, except I'm afraid she'll make us walk there instead of fly, in order to reduce our carbon footprint," Gunnar said. The expression on his face told Chris he might actually try to walk if Hazel required it.

"Does anyone have a guess where Buckley is?" Ivan asked, bringing the conversation back around. "Chris and I asked around at the market today, and no one has seen him recently."

"No idea, I swear on Hazel's head," Gunnar said.

"So that wasn't you last night?" Ivan asked. "We heard engines and gunfire."

"We didn't hear anything," Susie exclaimed.

"That does not come as a surprise, Mom," said Chris.

"No, we went bowling," Tyrone answered. "Massive bowling alley, forty lanes. Next year we're going to try and convince Dutch, Foster, Becca—Foster's sister—and Hazel to come down over winter break. Go to the Grand Canyon, visit Joshua Tree."

While the rest of the table talked about what there was to do and the best time of year to do it, Chris made a quick phone call.

"What the hell, Hatch. You are on vacation, why are you calling?" McBride demanded.

"Let me explain."

Five minutes later, McBride was still grumbling but less loudly and he'd agreed to reach out to his connections at Fish and Game. With a little luck and planning, the missing Cleevus Buckley would be located and would no longer be in business.

"I can't even force you to go on vacation without you finding a way to work."

"It's a knack," Chris said. "What can I say?"

"A knack," McBride repeated. "Well, get off the phone and enjoy the rest of your time off."

"Over and out."

Everyone looked expectantly at Chris as he sat back down at the table. Feeling devilish, he turned to his mother. "I'd love some more lemonade. How did Ping-Pong go this morning?"

"Don't you dare, Christopher Anthony Hatch! You tell us right now what happened on that secret phone call!"

"McBride is on it. He'll let us—and by us, I mean me—know what he learns from Fish and Game, but he did a quick search and it looks like Buckley is a known problem, so getting a legal warrant won't be difficult. And with any luck, agents will catch up with him as well. Could be they find out what the gunfire was about too."

"That is great news," said Susie. "Does everyone else want more lemonade?"

There was a chorus of yesses and soon enough, everyone's glasses were full again.

"So," his mom said, settling back in her seat, "sweetie, what do you and Ivan have planned for the rest of your time here?"

THE NEXT MORNING, Chris still couldn't wrap his head around randomly hanging out with his parents and the ex-leader of a notorious motorcycle gang. Eventually, they'd finally made their excuses, said goodbye to Gunnar and Tyrone, and escaped back to Frank's house, leaving Susie and Lance to work on the 1500-piece vintage hummingbird jigsaw puzzle on their own.

To be fair, Ivan hadn't used the word escape—that was all on Chris. There was just only so much chitchat Chris could stand. And anyway, what did a DEA agent discuss casually with an ex-criminal? Gunnar was older than Chris by almost twenty years, but they'd been on opposite sides of the law for a great deal of Chris's career. The whole thing made him slightly uncomfortable.

Frank's air conditioning was humming along in the background, and the house was nice and cool. Back in the bedroom, Chris scraped a towel over his head, drying his hair after a much-needed shower. Ivan was still distractingly naked, sprawled on his front across the mattress as he pored over several guidebooks on the Grand Canyon. It was all very domestic and unreasonably pleasant.

Ivan looked up from his reading and caught Chris's eyes on him. He smiled.

"What?" Chris asked, instantly suspicious and mildly uncomfortable, as if he'd been caught stealing from a cookie jar.

"You make me happy," Ivan said. His green eyes sparkled.

"Mmph." Chris rolled his eyes. Although he had to admit that making Ivan happy was pretty much at the top of his to-do list. A list he hadn't realized he'd had until recently.

"I make you laugh. Which in turn makes you happy— because endorphins," Ivan said in a smug tone.

"Fucking endorphins."

With a chuckle, Ivan rolled over to sit at the edge of the mattress, patting the spot next to him. "Sit down."

Tossing the damp towel onto the dresser, Chris stepped over to the bed and lowered himself down.

"Fine, you make me laugh," he admitted. "Yes, I always look forward to seeing you around the office. I'm going to miss that." After returning to Frank's last night, Ivan had finally given him all the details about his request to transfer to Radisson's team in Portland and told him that, unless something came up, the transfer was likely to go through. "Hard to believe I make you happy though."

"Get used to it. Because I'm not going anywhere."

Ivan scooted even closer so that there was no space left between them. It had been a day and some change, and Ivan's body pressed against his was a habit he didn't plan on giving up. But they had plans, and staying in and engaging in the wild rumpus would mean they might not get to the canyon.

He leaned down, intending to grab his shorts from where he'd carelessly abandoned them on the floor the night before, when someone knocked on the front door.

"Oh my god, it's my mother. That's the only person it could be."

Sure enough, the knocking was followed by Susie's voice. "Are you lovebirds awake in there? Breakfast is ready at our pad!" His mother's voice, cheery as it always was. "Ivan, I found some more Chris pictures to show you. But we can save them for when you get back from your trip tonight."

"Oh my god," Chris moaned, cradling his head in his hands. "I don't know if I can stand this. Can't we pretend we broke up or something? The woman doesn't sleep! It's not even seven a.m. and she—"

"She loves you," Ivan reminded him. "Both of your parents do. And, no we can't pretend we broke up. Sorry, Dude, no can do. Can you imagine how sad Susie would be? And Lance too. Besides"—Ivan rubbed his belly—"I could do with something to eat before we leave. Worked up an appetite last night," he added with an evil grin.

Dropping his hands, Chris stared at Ivan, at the man he loved. "You are incorrigible."

"Sounds a lot better than being corrigible. Is it like being sheveled, as in un-disheveled? I've always wondered about those two words."

Chris squinted at Ivan, shaking his head. "You are the only person I know who would wonder about those two words which do not exist."

"Chris? Ivan?" His mom's voice was only slightly muffled by the thin front door.

"We'll be right there, Mom," Chris responded, willing Susie to get a clue.

"It stands to reason that, if incorrigible and disheveled exist, then there has to be a corrigible and sheveled. And also a gruntled."

"See you in a minute, boys."

"We better dress and get over there ASAP. Mom might resort to picking the lock or something like that to make sure we really are okay in here."

Chris stood up again to finish getting ready. Just how did one prepare for a day that would be spent with Ivan Morrison anyway?

"Are you okay?" Ivan asked abruptly, his words spilling out fast. "Are you okay with us?"

He sounded worried, which was so unlike the confident man Chris was familiar with that he paused with his shorts halfway up his legs. Hastily, he finished pulling them up before stepping over so he was standing between Ivan's knees.

"Yes," Chris said once he had Ivan's undivided attention. "I am absolutely okay with this, with us."

"So, this was a successful wooing? Thing is, I don't know if I can work up the courage to try something like this again." Ivan swiped at his forehead as if he was sweating bullets.

"You don't have to, I promise. But why would you be worried? You're Ivan the Undaunted."

"Yeah, well." Ivan shot him a weak grin. "It's a lot of smoke and mirrors if you want to know the truth. But"—he squinted in what Chris supposed was an attempt to look threatening—"don't tell anyone."

"What will you do if I share your little secret?" Chris teased. He stepped back to grab a t-shirt.

Ivan looked thoughtful as he reached over, snagged his own shorts, and pulled them on before answering. "It'll be bad for sure." Done with fastening his waistband, Ivan's big hands landed on Chris's hips and he tugged him closer. "I might have to ravish you."

Chris's dick twitched, but he reminded himself that his parents were waiting for them.

"Oh, ravishing. I like the sound of that." Chris waggled his eyebrows this time, earning a smile from Ivan. He'd do just about anything to make Ivan smile at him like that.

"Anytime, baby, any time."

"Anytime except now." Chris moved away slightly. "Mom has breakfast ready and we need to go if we want to hit the road."

"Just know there's a possible ravishing in your future."

"Possible, huh?" Grinning, Chris bent and brushed his lips across Ivan's. Anything more and they wouldn't make it to breakfast *or* the Grand Canyon.

EPILOGUE

New Year's Eve

HATCH

"WHAT FRESH FUCKING hell is this? How do you wear these monkey suits every day of your fucking life?" Ivan complained.

Suppressing a grin, Chris paused mid-unpacking and closet organizing to glance across the suite at his boyfriend.

"Quit twitching and fiddling, you look just fine."

Unsurprisingly to Chris, Ivan Morrison did look fine. Better than fine. Remarkably fine. He filled out a suit extraordinarily well. Especially since Chris was more accustomed to the leathers and denim that Ivan normally wore.

They'd been invited and had obviously accepted an invitation from Andy Radisson to attend an exclusive New Year's Eve party being held at a mansion on the Olympic Peninsula. This was their first formal event as a couple, and Ivan had been nervous since the envelope had arrived in the mail.

After reading the invite and the black-tie dress code, Ivan had announced that The Ugly Suit Warehouse would be fine for what he needed, thankyouverymuch. But Chris had put his foot down, and now he was experiencing firsthand just how good Ivan Morrison looked in a suit altered to fit him properly. Ivan had done something to his hair too, so it didn't look like he'd recently stuck a knife into a light socket. He still preferred it to the cut from last winter. Luckily, Ivan's current role on Radisson's team did not require any undercover work, so overly short hairstyles were a thing of the past.

Ignoring Chris's instructions, Morrison tugged the sleeves of his dress jacket down over his wrists again. The third time in forty seconds. This was followed by a roll of his shoulders and neck, as if the suit was actively strangling him.

"Haven't you had to wear one of these sometime in your life?" Chris asked.

"At my dad's funeral."

Well.

There was a conversation stopper if Chris had ever heard one before. But... it wasn't going to work on him. He'd known Morrison for years, and the one person he never had anything nice to say about was his father. His family, as a whole, was quite literally a dead topic.

"So what? Get over it. This time it's for a good cause." Plus, he'd wangled an invitation for Susie and Lance too, a fact Chris had managed to keep from his boyfriend. Their presence would be a surprise, and one Chris hoped would please Ivan.

It would, he knew it would.

Ivan shot him a scowl. "Fine." The look might have made another man nervous, but Chris knew Ivan well, and he was really a big softy who would gladly watch Taylor Swift videos with scared teens and rescue bedraggled kittens from trees if that was what was needed.

"That's right. *Fine.* It's fine, and you're not missing the fundraising part of this because you don't like suits. Besides," Chris added truthfully, "you look amazing."

Ivan looked away and down the broad expanse of his chest all the way to his freshly shined leather shoes. At over six foot four inches, Morrison had a long way to look.

"I feel like an idiot. Next party, you have to wear leathers and combat boots," Ivan grumbled. Chris managed not to point out that this was Ivan's boss's party and thus his rules, not McBride's. Lifting his head again, Ivan shot Chris an appraising look. "You'd look pretty all right too, maybe even fool some old-timers. But"—he wrinkled his nose as he turned back to his reflection—"you'd have to do something about the Ken hair."

"Ken hair?" Reflexively, Chris lifted a hand and touched his head. "What's wrong with my style?"

Dark eyebrows rose toward his hairline as Morrison turned away from the floor-length mirror to move across the room toward Chris.

"Style? You never let your hair have any fun," he said, reaching out to brush his fingers through Chris's carefully coiffed hair.

"Knock it off." Chris pushed Morrison's hand away. "Now I have to fix it again."

"You really don't," Morrison assured him. "Messy gives you a sort of devil-may-care look. Not the one you normally have. You know, the one that makes it look like you're constipated. I dunno," he added thoughtfully, "maybe you are? Do you eat enough fiber?"

"Jesus Christ. We are not having this conversation." Ivan did most of the cooking, so he knew exactly what Chris ate.

"So, you *are* constipated?"

"No, Ivan, I am not constipated. Are you happy now?"

Ivan shot him a toothy grin, the one that told Chris he'd been teased and fallen for it. Ivan Fucking Morrison, whom Chris loved with all of his grinchy heart. Every last bit of it.

Chris glanced at his watch, a Rolex he'd bought himself a few years ago. Not top-of-the-line, but it pleased him and looked good with his suit, as if he was some kind of success and not just a DEA lifer. One who now had Ivan Morrison in his bed every night.

"It's time to go downstairs for predinner drinks and appetizers." Glancing up, he caught Ivan's assessing gaze. The amusement that sparked in the dark brown depths had Chris clearing his throat. "Promise you'll behave yourself," he said in a firm tone. "No hard-ons."

"Oohhh." Morrison waggled his eyebrows this time in a manner that could only be understood as suggestive. "Going all daddy and stern on me now? You know I love it when you take a firm hand."

Chris shut his eyes for a brief moment and bit his lips together in an effort not to laugh. He knew better than to respond. Whatever he said now, Ivan would *absolutely* take it the *absolutely* wrong way and twist his words into something that would one hundred percent give both of them semis. They'd argue and be late getting downstairs, and that couldn't happen. He wanted to get down early and watch all the other guests as they arrived. He wanted to see Ivan's expression when he spotted Susie and Lance waiting for them in the dining room.

"Ivan," he muttered warningly.

Morrison snapped to attention, spine as straight as a soldier's, and stuck his elbow out.

"What's that for?" Chris asked, staring at the appendage.

"Why shouldn't I offer you my arm?" Ivan demanded.

"Ivan, I am not an infirm senior citizen."

"Yeah, I know that," Morrison replied slowly as if Chris was a bit slow, "and we aren't married either. But we could be married if we wanted to, so there."

So there? Really?

"I'm not hanging on to your arm. I'm forty-four, not eighty-four."

Taking one last look at himself in the mirror, Chris started toward the door and, more importantly, the stairs down to the lobby. He had a plan, and standing here debating random shit with Ivan would not keep him on track.

Footsteps sounded behind him. Chris opened their room door and motioned for Ivan to go first. But he knew Ivan would get the last word in, he always did.

As Ivan passed him, he leaned in close enough that Chris could feel the exhale of his words against his cheek.

"Not eighty-four, but aged like a fine whisky—just how I like you."

With that parry, he swanned by Chris on his way to the landing. Resisting the almost overwhelming urge to drag Ivan back into the suite and throw him onto the bed, Chris followed his boyfriend down the staircase.

IVAN

OLYMPIC MANOR. *What a fucking gig.*

Upon arrival, Ivan had avoided looking around too much. He was still reeling from the invitation to the hoity-toity extravaganza and he didn't want to look like a hick—even if he was one. The party was for a good cause, funding safe houses for sex trafficking survivors, but Ivan wasn't used to rubbing shoulders with the brass.

Could a person reel for weeks?

He could and he had. Was still. *Whatever.* He glanced around again.

Olympic Manor had been built in the 1930s, supposedly by one of the set designers who'd worked on Errol Flynn's *Robin Hood*. Once it was finished, Flynn had stayed there, too. Morrison was fairly sure the term "over the top" had been coined by the architect. It was all glitz and velvet. Rumor had it there was a Picasso around somewhere.

Slowly, Ivan descended the staircase with Chris right behind him—not holding his elbow.

"Hurry up. What the fuck are you doing?" Chris hissed.

"Making an entrance? Isn't that what we're supposed to do?"

"Jebezzus, Morty, and the Hellish host," Chris muttered so only Ivan could hear him.

"Excuse me?" Ivan paused on the last stair to look over his shoulder at the love of his life.

"Oh." Chris looked a little sheepish. "Something my mom says. I've always thought it was hilarious, seemed appropriate here. Doesn't it look like Charles Dickens might show up?"

"What does that have to do with me taking the stairs slowly? I need to know more about this. How did I not know about this saying until tonight?" Ivan demanded.

"Because," Chris said firmly, "I don't need Mom to give you any more encouragement."

Ivan took the last step down into the red velvet hell that was the enormous lobby. "I'll just call and ask her about it."

He went to pull his cell phone out, but Chris stopped him before he entered the dining room.

"Do not call my mother tonight."

Just then a posh-looking guy around Chris's age emerged from the bar adjacent to the lobby. Skinny and with a pinched face, he looked like the kind of person who toadied for rich bastards. Fucking Paulter.

"Why is he here?" Ivan said under his breath, setting aside the *don't call Susie* command for a moment. "Hasn't he been banished?"

"Behave," Chris growled. "Lots of people were invited, and you probably won't like all of them. And no, Paulter has unfortunately not been banished."

"Ooh. Bossy again. You know that just makes me want to be bad. Let's go back upstairs."

"Come on." Chris tugged at him. "I'll buy you a drink. Would you like a glass of champagne?"

The bar looked like what Ivan imagined a speakeasy might have. In fact, he'd read that there had been a speakeasy on the premises in the thirties, but surely it hadn't been just off the lobby?

The walls were covered with red and gold-striped wallpaper and elaborate art nouveau-style sconces with bulbs that looked like candles, hung every few feet. The mahogany bar took up most of a wall, with liquor of all kinds displayed behind it and glassware hanging from racks set into the ceiling.

"Wow."

"I thought you might think this was cool. Very *Casablanca*. Two glasses of champagne, please," Chris said to the bartender.

"My favorite movie," Ivan said.

Chris was fumbling around in his pocket, maybe looking for his wallet.

"We can just put this on our room."

"Duh," Chris responded. Instead of his wallet, he set a small velvet box on the dark bar top and pushed it toward Ivan with his index finger.

"What's this?" Ivan asked, his heart pounding against his ribs. Where had all the oxygen gotten to? He needed some about now.

The pocket-sized bar suddenly seemed too small. And too quiet—as if he had cotton in his ears.

Chris half smiled at him. "You're a smart guy, Ivan. What do you think it is?"

The bartender set two glasses of champagne down in front of them. Ivan resisted the urge to toss the bubbly back immediately and order another one.

"Ivan," Chris said so quietly he almost couldn't hear him.

"Um, yes?"

He raised his eyes from the tiny box to Chris's face. Holding his gaze, Chris flipped the box open. Nestled inside was a simple silver band—surely it wasn't platinum? Jesus Christ, what if he lost it?

"Ivan Morrison." Chris drew his name out just how Ivan liked it. "Would you do the honor of marrying me?"

"Me?" Ivan squeaked.

Chris smiled and very much invaded Ivan's personal space so they were only a few inches apart.

"Yes, Ivan. You."

For once in his life, Ivan didn't know what to say. No, not true. He knew what to say, and he very much wanted to say it, but the lump in his throat became a boulder and he had to force out the word.

"Yes."

"Yes?"

The world came rushing back and so did Ivan's words. "Yes, boss, I will join you in an unholy union." Surely, it wouldn't be holy, that would be ridiculous.

"Hold your hand out." Carefully, Chris removed the ring from the box and slid it onto Ivan's ring finger.

"It fits," he said, mildly surprised.

"Of course it fits," Chris scoffed. "I can actually do secret stuff too, you know."

"Oh, you can, can you?" Ivan looked down at the ring glittering on his finger. "I never thought I'd want to get married."

"Yeah, me neither. That is, I never thought *I'd* want to get married," Chris clarified. "But here we are, and I find myself wanting to make it legal—you and me. Besides, it gives Mom a new passion."

"Your parents know?" Ivan loved Susie and Lance, but he still had a smidgeon of doubt that they would want him as a son-in-law. "They approve?"

"Why don't you ask them yourself?"

Chris shifted and Ivan looked down the bar to the end of the narrow room. Susie and Lance were sitting at a round table tucked into the corner. Their enormous smiles said everything, but that didn't stop Susie from calling out over the ragtime that was playing overhead, "Welcome to the family, Ivan!"

With yet another smile, Chris brushed his lips across Ivan's, "I love you. Let's go have champagne with Mom and Dad before we bid on that trip to Iceland."

Chris went to move, but Ivan grabbed his arm to stop him. "I love you, Christopher Anthony Hatch, and I'm never going to let you forget it."

"Is that a promise or a threat?" Chris asked, his sly grin tempting Ivan.

"Oh, that's a promise *and* a threat."

IF YOU ENJOYED *SNOWBIRDS*, I would greatly appreciate if you would let your friends know so they can get to know Chris Hatch and Ivan Morrison. Please share on Facebook, TikTok, instagram, wherever you like to shout about great books and best of all, leave a review!

If you haven't read the Reclaimed Hearts series yet start with Adverse Conditions and keep going! You'll get to dive into the small town of Cooper Springs and meet the quirky folks who live and love there.

KEEP up-to-date with new releases and sales, *The Highway to Elle* hits your in-box approximately every two weeks, sometimes more sometimes less. I include deals, freebies and new releases as well as a sort of rambling running commentary on what *this* author's life is like. I'd love to have you aboard! I also have a reader group called the Highway to Elle, come say hi!

ABOUT ELLE

Writing inclusive romance featuring complex characters and a unique sense of place is my happy place. The characters start out broken, and maybe they're still a tad banged up by the end, but they find the other half of their hearts and ALWAYS get their happily ever after.

In 2017 I pressed the publish button for the first time and never looked back—making this the longest period of time I've stuck with a job--in my entire life. Currently, there are over thirty-five Elle Keaton books available for you to read or listen to.

I love cats and dogs. Star Wars and Star Trek. Pineapple on pizza, and have a cribbage habit my husband encourages. Connecting with readers is very important to me. If you are so inclined, join my newsletter, The Highway to Elle, and keep up to date with everything Elle related.

Including, but not limited to, 'where are my glasses?', and 'why are there cats?'. I can also be found on Facebook, Instagram and occasionally TikTok.

AFTERWORD

This is a work of fiction, created without use of AI technology. Any names, characters, places or incidents are products of the author's imagination and used in a fictitious manner. Any resemblance to actual people, places, or events is purely coincidental or fictional.

Elle Keaton's creative body of work cannot be used in any manner for the purpose of training AI.

The author, Elle Keaton, supports the right of humans to control their artistic works. No part of this book has been created using AI-generated images or narrative, as known by the author. The primary style sources used in the writing of this book are the online versions of the Merriam-Webster Dictionary and The Chicago Manual of Style. Due to their inherent limitations for fiction-writing and the author's personal style choices, there are instances where other style guide rules have been consistently applied. Region-based idioms, age- or era-appropriate slang, UK spelling and style rules, and other deviations based on specific dialects may inform some of these choices. Should you have questions, please contact the author at: dirty dogpress@gmail.com